'Thanks for t
confidence.'

Glancing up into his face, Claire saw, not the mature man she was half afraid of, but the serious surgeon who had doubts in spite of his experience, and she knew she would never be afraid of him again. Mark, sensing a change in her, knew he must not take advantage of this softening towards him, but it didn't still the desire that heated his body.

Dear Reader

Although we don't move out of England this month, we do tackle some quite different subjects. In THE STORM AND THE PASSION by Jenny Ashe, Emma has a moral question to face, while Kate in SOMEBODY TO LOVE by Laura MacDonald wonders if she can cope with a short-term affair. In TO DREAM NO MORE by Patricia Robertson, Claire has to overcome fear, while Briony in VET IN POWER by Carol Wood has to overcome the bitterness generated by the feud between her family and Nick's. Problems galore—will our heroines win through?

The Editor

Patricia Robertson has nursed in hospitals, in District Health, and abroad. Now retired, she is incorporating this past experience in her Medical Romances. Widowed with two daughters, her hobbies are gardening, reading and taking care of her Yorkshire terriers. She lives in Scotland.

Recent titles by the same author:

HEART IN JEOPARDY
YESTERDAY'S MEMORY

TO DREAM NO MORE

BY

PATRICIA ROBERTSON

MILLS & BOON LIMITED
ETON HOUSE   18–24 PARADISE ROAD
RICHMOND   SURREY   TW9 1SR

First published in Great Britain 1993
by Mills & Boon Limited

© Patricia Robertson 1993

Australian copyright 1993
Philippine copyright 1993
This edition 1993

ISBN 0 263 78189 5

Set in 10 on 11 pt Linotron Times
03-9308-57441

Typeset in Great Britain by Centracet, Cambridge
Made and printed in Great Britain

CHAPTER ONE

IT WAS a man's face, white and threatening, looming above her. It had the clear-cut lines of a statue, the nose straight, the mouth perfectly shaped, the lips neither too thick nor too thin, and the eyes — the eyes were blue and cold, as dead as alabaster. The hair was dark with silver strands threaded throughout. It would have been a beautiful face if there had been even a little life in the eyes. Instead, the impassive, hard features held a menace that terrified Claire. It was not the face alone which frightened her. The white surrounding it, tinged with blue, gave it a disembodied appearance, a ghostly quality which added to her fear.

Claire woke. Her body was trembling, her eyes staring, her face wet with perspiration. Her strange surroundings did nothing to allay her fears, so she was disorientated and too frightened to move.

Then the friendly sound of milk bottles clinking lifted her out of her nightmare. She reached for the glass on her bedside table and drank; the water moistened her dry mouth, wetted her parched lips. She took a deep breath and swung her legs over the side of the bed. The fingers of her alarm clock pointed to six. Crossing to the window, she threw aside the curtains and with them banished her dream. It was going to be a hot day.

She smiled as she looked out at the park opposite to her block of flats, and her spirit lifted. It was wonderful to be back in Whiteleigh-on-Sea.

Claire ran her fingers through her short fair hair, flicking her fringe back into place, and wondered if she would ever be rid of her nightmare, but it was only for a moment. She had had it since childhood, and as she had grown older it had troubled her less. Any change or emotional upset caused it to recur. She should have expected her move to Whiteleigh to bring it back.

But it was always there waiting, as it were, in the wings, waiting to catch her off guard. It had resulted in her becoming reserved and cool towards those she came in contact with. Only the sick, and especially children, could break through this barrier she had erected. Only with them and members of her own family could she be truly natural.

Claire sighed. She went to have a bath, and as she soaked with the bubbles up to her chin her finely boned face became serious. Would this move to Whiteleigh solve her other problem? Would it force her cousin Steven to accept that she did not love him?

The steam hung in drops on her fair eyebrows, and as she drew them together in a frown they fell off like raindrops.

Her mother had died tragically and Claire, a child of three, who had been with her, had survived. Her father was an oil man who travelled all over the world, and he had left Claire with Marion West, Claire's aunt. Steven was her son. His father was a successful architect, and the family lived in Surrey. Marion had been delighted to take Claire, she had always wanted a daughter and, as she was unable to have any more children, Claire had been made very welcome.

Steven was two years older than Claire, and she had trailed after him everywhere. He enjoyed her hero-worship and played up to it.

Each summer they had holidayed in Whiteleigh, her father joining them when he could. Claire adored Alan Forrest, and there was a strong bond between them which Steven resented.

As they grew older, Steven had tried a succession of jobs which all failed because he lacked motivation.

When their grandmother had died and left Claire and Steven a substantial income, he did not try any more. Claire, who had been training to become a nurse at the time, continued to complete her course, and when qualified went on to take her Sick Children's Certificate.

She could still hear Steven saying, 'I don't know why you need to work. You could marry me and have a good time.'

She had laughingly refused and told him she was taking a job. 'I don't love you, Steven, at least not in that way.' She had stopped trailing after him when she went to boarding-school.

When her father had died six months previously, Steven had intensified his pursuit of her until she was so fed up that she said,

'I'm leaving London. You don't love me, Steven. You just want me because I don't want you.' For a slim fragile blonde, she could be firm when she chose.

Steven had shrugged. 'Oh, well, perhaps a spell away from me will change your mind.'

Claire had not bothered to reply. She knew it would be useless. Steven would believe what Steven wanted to believe. Claire had chosen Whiteleigh because of its happy associations.

A nursing agency had accepted her. She did not want to be restricted, and as an agency nurse she would be free to accept or refuse cases as she wished.

They were short-staffed on the children's ward at Whiteleigh General Hospital, and the agency had asked Claire to accept the post of temporary staff nurse on that ward. She had agreed, and was due to start that morning.

The bath water had become cold, and this drew her from her reverie. It must be late. She climbed out of the bath, nearly slipping in her haste. The bedside clock told her it was seven-thirty. Years of practice at dressing quickly enabled her to be in her uniform, to have had a cup of coffee and be out of the flat by a quarter to eight.

The sun was shining in her eyes as she took her seat behind the wheel of her red Mini. She lowered the visor and started the engine. Turning left at the end of the road, she was in the High Street, and her face lit with pleasure when she saw the familiar shops. She felt she had come home.

Ten minutes later she turned into the hospital car park. As she locked the car door, she looked across at the red brick building which had been erected just before the Second World War. It was not a teaching hospital and did not have a medical school attached to it, but its reputation was good, and the children's ward was well used, especially during the summer months. Whiteleigh was a popular holiday town.

Claire entered the hospital and followed the signs directing her to the administration section. She was just about to open the glass door leading to the office when a man's reflection appeared from behind her, the glass acting as a ghostly mirror.

Her hand on the door-handle turned to ice. The man reflected was the man in her dream. Her mouth dry, she swung round, fear in her eyes, but there was no one there. Shocked, she wondered if she was becoming paranoid.

A voice from her other side said, 'Can I help you, Nurse?'

Claire turned, forcing herself to relax. The homely face of a middle-aged ward sister looking at her kindly helped. The numbness she had felt at seeing the apparition left her and she smiled.

'I was told to report to the senior nursing officer,' she said. 'I'm the agency nurse, Claire Forrest.'

The sister smiled. 'I'll take you with me. You're to work on my ward — I'm Sister Jessie Watson.' Her eyes were mischievous as she said, 'I'll tell Mrs Godfrey I kidnapped you.'

Claire laughed. She knew in advance when they had reached the children's ward. Large pictures depicting Disney characters could be seen through the portholes of the swing doors, and the sound of children's voices could be heard through them.

Jessie Watson gestured for Claire to precede her. Just inside the doors, she clapped her hands for silence. Babies in cots and children ageing from three to eight looked towards the sound, except for a one-year-old who did not stop crying. There were smiles on the small faces as they looked at the ward sister.

Jessie Watson beamed at her small charges. 'Children, I want you to meet Nurse Forrest, who's come to look after you.'

Bright faces, worried faces, sad faces and cautious ones examined Claire solemnly. Claire smiled and their little faces relaxed, their small hands unclenched and they beamed. They had decided that she was not a threat. One small child with his leg in plaster hobbled towards her and held out a picture of a train he had been crayoning.

Claire crouched down to his level and putting an arm around his thin shoulders said, 'That's very good.'

Spontaneously, the child gave her a wet kiss.

Jessie smiled her approval and said, 'We have open visiting,' gesturing to one of the mothers who had arrived early. 'Unfortunately, though, quite a few of our patients are holiday accidents and the parents can't stay.' She nodded to the still crying baby.

In the office, a big observation window ran the length of one wall. 'Nurse Brown,' Jessie was adressing a young nurse with a pleasant face, 'please go and give Baby Morton a cuddle. I'll give you the report later.'

The nurse smiled and left the office. Claire could see her hurrying towards the baby.

Jessie introduced Claire to the staff, who were composed of State-Enrolled nurses and auxiliaries.

After the report had been taken and the night staff had left, Jessie detailed her nurses their duties.

'Be particularly careful, Nurse Jeffries,' she instructed a tall angular girl with red hair, 'with Billy Johnson when you feed him.' She glanced at Claire. 'Billy had his cleft lip repaired when he was a baby. Now he's eighteen months old he's to have his cleft palate done. Mr Stanger has his operation scheduled for Wednesday.'

Claire nodded.

'I'll go through the case histories with you as you're acting as staff nurse while you're here so that our consultant, Mark Stanger, won't be able to catch you out.' Jessie grinned broadly. 'It's not as bad as it sounds,' she said, seeing Claire's frown. 'It's just that he's very efficient and expects everyone else to be so too.'

Claire had met consultants like that before and found the best way to deal with them was to be ahead of them, so she listened intently to everything Jessie was telling her.

The last case-note was returned to the trolley. Jessie said, 'Now I'll put faces to the names,' smiling as she ushered Claire out of the office.

The noise in the ward was louder than when they had been in earlier. Breakfast seemed to have given those almost recovered extra energy.

'Come here, Kevin,' an exasperated auxiliary's voice rose an octave. 'Give me that plate.'

The young boy with his leg in plaster who had shown his picture to Claire seemed to have undergone a character change. The angel face that had kissed Claire's was alive with mischief as he scuttled out of the auxiliary's reach.

Jessie and Claire were trying to intercept the child when a deep voice from behind them said, 'Kevin!'

It was enough. Kevin smiled sheepishly, hobbled up to the auxiliary and handed her the plate.

Claire caught a glimpse of a white coat as she turned. A redheaded man with a stethoscope peeping out of his pocket, a bright red and green tie glaring between his lapels, smiled at her.

'He's a proper little menace, isn't he, Sister?' he said, grinning at Jessie.

'He can be a little highly-strung at times,' was the understated reply.

'He'll crack that plaster if he isn't careful.' The young doctor was shaking his head.

'This is Ronnie North, our house surgeon,' Jessie introduced the young man, who was giving Claire an admiring glance.

Claire's face was expressionless and Ronnie's eyebrows rose. Turning to Jessie, he said,

'I came early to let you know the big chief's coming at nine to do the round. He's to give a talk to the police about abused children at eleven.' He winked at Claire and left with a smile.

'Don't pay any attention to Ronnie.' Jessie's voice had a smile in it. 'It's all show with him. He's very good with the children.'

Claire blushed.

'You'll find it a lot quieter here than the children's ward at your training hospital,' Jessie said when they had returned to the office. 'We're not equipped for intensive care; we don't have a unit here. Anything that requires specialised treatment is taken to London.' She pushed a strand of grey hair under her cap. 'Mr Stanger operates once a week. Sometimes he'll use a bed for a child who would have to wait for one in the London hospital.'

Jessie paused and Claire thought she should say something, so she said, 'I see.'

'We'll do the medicines together first.' Jessie smiled.

'Then you'll have an idea of who has what, and afterwards you can take a look around the ward and get your bearings.'

'Thanks.'

The medicines were soon done. Claire was poking about in the treatment-room, and as her hands were busy her mind wondered about that reflection she had seen in the glass. It must have been her subconscious playing tricks, she decided, following her dream last night.

She was just looking for the small splints when one of the nurses, a woman in her thirties, put her head round the door.

'Sister wants you for the round, Staff.' Anne Brown's face was as plain as her name, and her kind eyes were humorous and her bearing confident. 'Mr Stanger's arrived and doesn't like to be kept waiting.' She grinned, and Claire smiled back.

The treatment-room was next to the office, and, even though Claire left immediately, Sister Watson was already in the ward with the doctors. Claire could see the backs of their white coats and recognised Ronnie North's red head through the porthole of the ward's door.

It was not until she went in that she saw the other man with him, and even then she did not have a clear view of him. He was holding the child due for repair of the cleft palate in his arms. The child's head was obscuring the doctor's, but she heard his voice, soothing and pleasant say,

'Hi, there, Billy.'

It was as Claire came round to Jessie's right-hand side that she saw the doctor's face and felt the blood drain from her own, for the man who glanced towards her was the man in her dream.

CHAPTER TWO

HER sharp intake of breath went unnoticed. Billy, however, sensing her disquiet, howled.

Claire was held in that half-world between reality and nightmare. The doctor, frowning with displeasure at her upsetting the child in his arms, was indentical in every way to the man who had haunted her since childhood. The straight nose, the perfectly shaped mouth, the hair black with touches of grey—even the eyes were the same blue, and they were looking at her with the same cold expression.

'Apparently Billy doesn't like your new staff nurse, Sister,' he said, his eyes narrowing.

Claire gripped the sides of the cot to steady herself, and was grateful for the unfairness of his words, for they jolted her out of her shock.

'Billy's not used to Staff Nurse Forrest yet, Mr Stanger,' said Jessie, concerned at how pale Claire had become.

Jessie's excusing Claire roused the fair girl's spirit. She was not going to let this man think that Billy was afraid of her, so she approached the doctor, even though her skin contracted with fear the nearer she drew to him. Ignoring his expression of disapproval, she held out her arms to the child and smiled a smile that had won many children's hearts when she was in training. It was loving, kind and gentle. Her blue eyes, so like the doctor's in colour, were as warm as the sun on the sea, and the child stretched out his small hands eagerly.

Mark was impressed and handed Billy into the blonde girl's arms. 'Hmm,' the sound was more a grunt

13

than a growl. He turned to Jessie. 'Has the mother used the elbow restraints yet, Sister?'

Jessie nodded. 'Yes, Mr Stanger. And we've applied them for a time so that he won't be frightened after the operation. The mother's been feeding him as well.'

Mark nodded. 'Good—good.'

Claire hung back, cuddling Billy, finding comfort in the small arms round her neck and the warmth of his body.

Gradually the nightmare feeling subsided as common sense told her that the man now crouching beside Barry was not her Nemesis, but just someone who looked like him.

Claire put Billy back in his cot and joined the others, but she could not stop her heart from beating faster, nor prevent her skin from becoming clammy.

'Well, Barry, home for you today.' The big man was crouching beside a six-year-old. Mark Stanger glanced up at Jessie. 'I've written to his doctor and spoken to his mother.' Barry was playing with the doctor's University tie, one Claire recognised as belonging to a famous London hospital.

'No more falling out of trees and cracking your skull next time you're on holiday, young man.' Mark smiled and patted Barry's head lightly.

The smile relaxed the stern lines on the doctor's face. It made him look younger, happier, and Claire let out a breath of relief. He could not possibly be the man in her dream, he was too vital, too alive.

As the round progressed, Claire studied Mark Stanger. He had the knack of being able to descend to each child's level both mentally and physically, and was obviously dedicated. And yet Claire could not rid herself of her unease. The coming to life of the man she was so afraid of was alarming, and she had difficulty concentrating on the ward round.

'Staff!' Mark Stanger's imperious voice cut through

her mental numbness. 'Don't you usually answer a question from the ward consultant?'

Claire looked at him with dull eyes which to him seemed impudent, and when she did not apologise, her mouth being too dry, his face became pale with anger. 'Sister! I'd like to see this nurse in your office after the round.'

It was the disappointed expression on Jessie Watson's face and not the doctor's words that blew Claire's numbness away. She was appalled that she had let the friendly ward sister down, but her mouth was still too dry to speak. She expected Jessie to send her to the office now, but Jessie just frowned, and the round continued.

Children, ever sensitive to change amongst the adults upon whom they depended, stared at Claire, some of them with apprehension, but she felt one small hand creeping into hers, and looking down saw the large almost black eyes of a little Jamaican boy gazing trustfully up at her. She knew he was Sammy Longston from Jessie's report.

Claire smiled and, crouching, put her arm about him. She did not see Mark glance briefly at her bent figure and so missed the puzzled expression that passed fleetingly over his face.

Keeping hold of Sammy's hand for the rest of the round, she kept smiling down at him, but missed none of the changes in treatment ordered by the consultant.

They were standing at the ward door, the round finished, when Mark Stanger said, smiling down at the boy still holding Claire's hand, 'We seemed to have missed you, Sammy.'

Ignoring Claire, he said to Jessie, 'I'd better have a look at his circumcision. How is it?'

'Fine, sir.' Jessie smiled down at the little black boy and reached for his hand, but Sammy would not let go of Claire's.

'Perhaps you'd take him to the treatment-room, then, Staff.' The cold voice matched the cold face in her dream.

But Claire had control of herself now and was able to reply steadily, 'Yes, sir,' her eyes as impersonal as his own.

Whatever was the matter with this girl? wondered Mark impatiently, annoyed that she made him feel as if he was in the wrong. She obviously had an affinity for children, and yet could not answer his simple question.

He turned to Jessie. 'I know you're busy, Sister. I'll manage.' His face relaxed into a very attractive smile which Claire did not see as she had her head bent talking in a low voice to Sammy.

'Thank you, Mr Stanger.' Jessie smiled. 'I'll see you in the office when you've finished.' She held the ward door open for Mark and Claire to pass through with their young charge.

In the treatment-room, Claire crouched down beside Sammy and put her arm round him. 'Well, Sammy?' Her voice had a husky, alluring quality which Mark wondered if the slim, fair nurse was aware of. There was an untouched air about her, and he suddenly knew what it was. This girl was a virgin. He was immediately intrigued.

'Will you show me your operation?' Claire asked the boy looking at her so trustfully. 'I promise not to touch it.'

The brown face beamed and the small hands pushed the cotton shorts down to expose the healed circumcision.

Mark crouched on the other side of the child, and Sammy's smile became even broader. The examination was over quickly, and Mark, grinning at the child, reached into his pocket and withdrew a sweet. It was red and shiny, wrapped in a see-through paper, and he handed it to Sammy.

'That's for being a good boy.' Mark's grin widened . 'You'll be going home tomorrow.'

Sammy leaned forward and kissed his lightly tanned cheek. Claire could not hide the expression of distaste that crossed her face. Mark saw it and was curious. He was fully aware of his sexual attraction and had found it troublesome at times, especially where the young nurses at his London hospital were concerned. They frequently developed crushes on him. This attractive girl's aversion for him he found interesting.

Mark stood up and looked down at Claire, who was still crouching beside the child. Sammy's dark skin emphasised the almost translucent whiteness of Claire's. His examination of her was intense, and her face tightened. She stood up and, holding Sammy's hand, looked pointedly at the door. Mark found himself opening it, and was astonished at the alacrity with which he did so.

'Thank you, sir,' said Claire in her best fee-paying-school voice, one she used to put people in their place.

Mark raised an eyebrow, but she ignored it. Sammy ran into the ward to join his friends, while Claire knocked on the office door. She could feel Mark standing behind her. She knew it was ridiculous, but her skin grew cold.

'Come in.' Jessie's cheerful voice drew a smile from Claire as she entered with Mark.

The light from the office window fell full upon the couple, accentuating their similarity — both their eyes were blue, and the difference in their hair colouring only emphasised how alike they were. They made an extremely handsome couple.

'Ronnie said he'd meet you in Outpatients before you go for your talk.' Jessie smiled. 'Would you like some coffee?' She pointed to the tray laid ready.

'No, thanks, Jessie. I'll get some later.'

Mark was surprised into admitting to himself that the girl standing so quietly beside him was disturbing him. Her closeness was rousing a desire to touch her, and somehow it disconcerted him. It was as if the attraction he felt was more than just sexual. He'd have to think about that.

'What about Staff Nurse Forrest?' Jessie reminded him, astonished that he should have forgotten to reprimand the agency nurse. Mark was a stickler for discipline.

He was at the door and glanced back. 'You can speak to Staff,' he said, not looking at Claire. 'I haven't time now,' and his white coat swished against the door as he went out.

Jessie's eyes were thoughtful as they rested on Claire. 'Well?' she said, raising her eyebrows. She gestured to the seat beside her desk. 'Sit down, Claire,' she said kindly. 'Now, do you have an explanation?'

What could Claire say? How could she tell Jessie about her dream? It would sound too fantastic, like a feeble excuse. So she said,

'No,' so quietly that Jessie almost did not hear her.

Claire's expression was bleak, and Jessie decided that the recent death of Claire's father must have been the reason. The agency had informed the SNO of Claire's bereavement.

She reached forward and patted Claire's hand.

'I understand,' she said gently. 'It takes time to recover after the death of a loved one.'

Claire realised to what the sister was alluding and felt awful, but all she could say was, 'Thank you for being so kind.'

'I'm sure it won't happen again.' Jessie beamed at her. 'Now have a cup of coffee and I'll show you the patients who need their dressings done, and we'll do them together so that you'll know just how Mr Stanger likes his dressings done.'

And so that I won't make any more mistakes, thought Claire.

The rest of the day was spent in finding her way around. She had lunch in the canteen, a pleasant place overlooking the hospital gardens of green lawns and flowerbeds bright with yellow and red antirrhinums.

She had finished her salad and was just raising a spoonful of ice-cream to her mouth when a voice said,

'Hi!' It was Ronnie North, and he sat down opposite to her.

Claire wished he had chosen somewhere else and said a cool 'Hello' to put him off, continuing to eat her ice-cream, intending to finish it as quickly as possible so that she could go.

'I bet the boss didn't tell you off,' said Ronnie, unabashed.

'How did you know?' Claire was surprised into replying.

An amused smile lit his eyes. 'I know he has a liking for blondes.'

'Really?' Her tone was cool.

He was eating steak pie. Finishing a mouthful, he grinned outrageously and said, 'I have a fancy for them as well.'

At another time Claire might have laughed, but the coming to life of her dream man was still with her, and she rose quickly, her chair falling backwards. She caught it before it reached the floor and set it on its feet.

'I have to go,' she said, too quickly.

Ronnie rose, blushing. 'I'm sorry if I've offended you,' he said.

Claire relented and smiled warmly. 'You haven't. It's just that it's my first day on a new ward, and you know what a strain that can be.'

He nodded and smiled, but she did not stay to chat.

Perhaps I should have encouraged him, she thought as she made her way back to the ward, but she knew she wouldn't. Her past experiences with young men had always ended in failure as soon as they kissed her. She froze and had come to believe that she was frigid.

She came off duty at six, more tired than she would have been normally, and was glad to climb into her Mini.

The traffic was heavy and delayed her so that her ten-minute drive became half an hour, and then she had to park the car further away from the flats than usual as her space had been taken.

She was still some way from the entrance when a man strode out of the block. It was Mark Stanger. He was too far away to see her, but she recognised him. She joined a bus queue to avoid him seeing her.

'You want this bus, miss?' An impatient voice spoke from behind her as the bus drew up.

'No, thanks,' she hastened to say, stepping out of the queue.

Why was her 'dream doctor'—she tried to think of him in a humorous way—coming out of her block of flats? Probably has a patient there, she decided, dismissing it.

CHAPTER THREE

CLAIRE'S shoulders drooped despondently as she approached the main door.

'Thought you'd never get here,' Steven drawled, coming up on her left-hand side.

Claire's mouth gaped. Then she flung her arms round him; the smell of his expensive aftershave clung to her cheek as they broke apart.

'Oh, Steve.' She smiled. It was good to see him even if he was a pest at times, and how debonair he was looking in grey trousers, a blue blazer and a striped scarf at his throat tucked into a white shirt. Steven never wore jeans and Claire had never seen him look scruffy. He was always impeccably dressed.

'Do I detect by this rapturous welcome that you're regretting your decision to move here?' There was a possessive smile on his face which wiped away her first flush of pleasure at seeing him.

'No,' was her emphatic reply. Her reasons for coming to Whiteleigh were the same, especially when she saw the gleam in his eye. Then she sighed. 'And yes,' she said, thinking of her 'dream doctor'.

'Aha!' Steven sounded triumphant. 'What's happened?'

Claire told him about the recurrence of her dream and about Mark Stanger.

Steven's eyes widened. He put his arm about her shoulders.

'Are you sure?' he asked. They were still standing at the main door.

'Of course I am.' She pulled away from his arm angrily.

Steven did not appear to notice her expression.

'I'm not surprised you had the dream again,' he said impatiently. 'You always do when you're under stress.' Then he grimaced. 'Perhaps you've persuaded yourself that this man looks like the man in your nightmare, but you're twenty-four now and this couldn't possibly be the same man. He'd be pretty old if he was.'

The anxiety that had pinched Claire's face as she had told him about seeing Mark Stanger lifted as Steven spoke the thoughts she had already had. She took a deep breath. 'Yes, of course.' She looked at her cousin and smiled. 'It's just that he's an exact look-alike.'

Steven was fed up with the subject and said, 'I'll take you out for a meal. It'll take your mind off your troubles.'

Claire sighed. 'Good. I'm starving,' she said, which wasn't quite true.

She took a step forward.

'Well, aren't you going to ask me up?' queried Steven, aggrieved.

'Yes, of course.' She really must concentrate on something other than her 'dream doctor'.

Once in the flat Steven flopped into the armchair.

'Wear that pale blue suit,' he called to her in the bedroom. 'I like you in that.'

Claire felt a touch of rebellion as she slipped on the shantung suit. She'd never liked it. It was cleverly cut and she did not wear a blouse under the jacket, but just a camisole top of the same colour. The straps slid off her shoulders; she'd been meaning to adjust them, but had forgotten. The silk material felt cold to her skin, and she shivered. She did not add any jewellery, feeling that the matching handbag and shoes were enough.

Surveying herself in the mirror, she pulled a face. It isn't really me, she thought, and gave her head a little shake. The fine blonde hair swished across her cheek, but she did not bother to smooth it into place before she went to join Steven.

Claire knew when her cousin had suggested this outfit that he would be taking her to the best restaurant in Whiteleigh, and so it proved.

He took her to a white sports car which was parked a block away. She raised her eyebrows, and seeing this he said,

'I parked it here deliberately. It would have spoilt my surprise visit if you'd seen it.'

Claire groaned inwardly, but smiled.

The restaurant was down by the harbour. A large window overlooked the yachts. Whiteleigh was a popular place for holiday sailors; its south coast position was convenient for those wishing to sail to France.

Steven had already booked a table. In fact, he must have made the reservation well in advance, for the Haven's reputation was widespread. This annoyed Claire. She had moved to Whiteleigh to escape Steven, not to have him pursue her.

She studied the large menu. The tensions of the day had taken away her appetite and she could not think what to choose.

Probably her lack of concentration made her look out of the window. Mark Stanger, in jeans and white T-shirt, a navy blue fisherman's sweater tied round his waist by the arms and white trainers on his feet, was standing on the stern of a white yacht throwing a rope to a slim young woman in skimpy pale blue shorts and matching sleeveless T-shirt. Claire could not see her face, just her fair hair, which was tied back in a ponytail. Must be one of his blondes, she mused, but she was relieved that the sight of Mark, this time, did not disturb her.

Lowering her menu, she said in an urgent whisper, 'There he is, Steven,' nodding towards the window.

'Who?' Steven looked in the direction she was indicating, but Mark had gone below.

'You just missed him.' Claire's tone was aggravated.

'Who?' Steven frowned.

'Mark Stanger.'

'Are you sure you didn't imagine you saw him?' Steven's expression was impatient.

Claire was stung into saying crossly, 'No, I didn't.'

'All right, all right, pet.' His conciliatory tone she found patronising, and she frowned. He glanced down at the menu. 'What are you having to eat?' He hoped the change of subject would distract her thoughts from this dream nonsense. He wanted her to concentrate on him.

Claire bent her head again to the menu and chose fruit juice followed by fresh salmon salad. Steven ordered melon, steak, and selected a bottle of wine. When the rosé was uncorked and he was tasting it, Claire said,

'Do you want me to drive if you're drinking?'

He frowned. It always aggravated him when she commented upon his drinking and driving.

'You know I can hold my liquor,' he retorted, affronted. 'It never affects my driving.'

'Still. . .' Claire persisted.

'Oh, shut up!' he snapped, his face dark with anger.

Rather than have a scene, which Steven was quite capable of making, Claire did just that, and they ate in silence.

They had just ordered their sweet when a couple arrived at the table adjacent to their own, and Claire's mouth gaped. It was Mark Stanger, in a well-cut grey suit, a white shirt and grey tie. With him was the blonde young woman — she could not have been more than eighteen — dressed in an expensive mini-skirt with matching top in a gold colour which combined with her now loose blonde hair should have made a sunshine picture, but the scar disfiguring the left side of her face spoiled the effect.

Mark was appalled at the expression on Claire's face. Surely a nurse, and a staff nurse at that, should have been able to control her horror at the sight of his companion?

Mark seated his companion with her back to the couple, arranging her seat so that it was more so. As he did this he was further shocked when he saw Claire bending towards her escort. It looked, to Mark's eyes, as if Claire was telling him about the girl, for the blond man turned his head in their direction.

Steven's eyes narrowed as he assessed Mark. He saw how attractive to women the handsome man was, and noted how the silver streaks amongst the dark strands of the big man's hair added to this attractiveness. Would the coming to life of Claire's dream release her dependency upon himself? He knew that he was the only man she was at ease with.

'You do believe me, Steven?' Claire looked anxiously at her cousin.

'As I've never seen the man in your dream, I suppose I must.' It was wicked of him to keep her off balance like this, but he wanted to keep his influence over her. 'Would you like to skip the sweet?'

Claire's uncertain expression, induced by Steven's words, was swept away by a determination that surprised even herself, for anything connected with her dream filled her with doubts.

'No,' she said firmly.

She found it difficult to understand why she knew she must stay, but finally convinced herself that the reason she was not rushing from the restaurant was because she knew she must put this fear of the man in her dream behind her. She must confront it, and finding someone who was identical with him would help.

She would not admit to herself that mixed with this

certainty was a feeling of sexual attraction for Mark. It was too bizarre.

Surreptitiously, she watched the couple. Apart from a cold glance in her direction Mark had not looked at her again; he was giving his companion his whole attention. This did not stop him from being aware of Claire, aware of every move she made, the way she ate her meringue glacé gracefully with an economy of movement. The fine lines of her face with its delicate beauty caught at his heart suddenly, so that he gasped, and the girl with him looked up from her grapefruit enquiringly. He was lost for an excuse to cover his sharp intake of breath, finally saying, 'The mayonnaise is rather tart.' He was eating a prawn cocktail.

As Claire left the restaurant she wondered who the young woman with Mark could be.

'I must say I wouldn't have taken a girl like that to the Haven,' Steven said, fastening his seatbelt.

His words shocked Claire from her own thoughts. She knew he was unmotivated, that he enjoyed his playboy life, but she had never thought of him as being quite that shallow.

'Like what?' Her voice was sharp as she asked the question she already knew the answer to, but she wanted to hear him say it.

Steven did not see the dislike on his cousin's face nor hear the timbre of her voice because he was changing up the gears and had over-reved the engine, but once in a quieter part of the town, he said,

'A scarred girl like that.' His voice held no compassion.

It took Claire until they had reached the flats to control her anger. Then she said, 'Perhaps he loves her,' in a cold voice as Steven opened the passenger door for her.

'You must be joking.' It was then that he saw her

shocked expression and said hastily, 'Well, I suppose it's possible,' but his words lacked conviction.

'Will you be staying the night?' Her tone was not inviting.

'No. I'm booked on the Dover ferry.' He glanced at his watch. 'Should make it if I hurry.'

The sky was still cloudless, so the daylight showed her face clearly—it was relieved.

He frowned. 'You'll miss me a bit, won't you?' he said, looking so forlorn that she said,

'Of course,' and threw her arms round his neck, even though she knew he was only putting it on.

Steven clasped her to him, savouring the delicate scent of her hair.

It was this picture that Mark saw as he parked his car a few yards away, and he was amazed to find the sight gave him pain. He had only met the girl that day, and he didn't think much of her attitude, judging by the way she had stared at Susie.

He climbed out of the car and slammed the door viciously.

It was this noise that broke Claire and Steven apart. Mark passed them without a glance and opened the door to the apartment block with his key.

'Must go, pet,' Steven said brightly. 'You'll be all right.'

Having seen Mark enter the building with a key, showing that he must live there, Claire would like to have asked Steven to stay, but she knew that he wouldn't have anyway. He was not noted for his unselfishness.

'Of course,' she said in her brightest voice.

Steven was relieved. There was a delicious, curvaceous blonde waiting for him in Paris, and he forgot he was supposed to be in love with Claire at that moment. He slipped behind the wheel and with a final wave was gone.

Claire let herself into the building. The flats were new, luxurious and expensive—just the sort of place a man like Mark Stanger would live, Claire thought, forgetting she lived there too.

She was about to pass him, thinking that the stairs would be preferable to sharing the lift with him, when he said as she drew level,

'I think you're a disgrace to the nursing profession.' His face had a light tan and it softened the angularity of his features, but did nothing for his eyes—they were cold.

Claire stood absolutely still, she didn't even blink. What little colour she had drained from her face and spots appeared before her eyes. She swayed and slipped to the floor in a faint. The emotional upheavals of the day coupled with the suddenness of his attack on her professional integrity had caught up with her.

A face was bending over her, a familiar face, but not a loved one. It was the face from her dream, but it puzzled her. There was more colour in its skin. Her fear was the same, though, and she screamed. Then the feel of the cold floor beneath her hands meant that she was not dreaming—it was real, and she shrank back, too terrified to scream.

'What the devil's wrong?' The solicitous expression on Mark's face changed to one of frustrated anger.

The sharpness of his words swept away Claire's feeling of being in a waking nightmare. It was Mark Stanger, and the realisation swept her with relief. 'I'm sorry,' she whispered.

'Here, let me help you to your feet.' His tone was gentler.

She knew it was ridiculous, but she could not bear to have him touch her so soon after mistaking him for the man in her dream, so she said,

'No, thanks. It's all right—I can manage.' But she

staggered, and he put his arm around her to steady her.

It was as if her body had contracted, almost as if it had lost its substance. I'm imagining it, Mark thought, but he knew instinctively that Claire was protecting herself, and from him — but why?

'My bag.' Her voice was a whisper.

He had to release her so that he could retrieve it. The softness of its leather was like her skin. He handed it to her. Claire backed away to stand by the lift, and Mark had the feeling that she had asked for her bag knowing he would have to let her go to pick it up. The annoyance he had felt when she had screamed at him stirred his curiosity. What was the reason for her acute aversion to him, and was this why he was attracted to her?

The lift doors opened before he could pursue his thoughts further, and a couple stepped out.

'What floor?' Mark asked not unkindly as they stepped inside.

'Second, please.' Claire's voice was stronger now.

She stood as far away from him as the confined space allowed, but, even so, she felt claustrophobic, and was glad when the doors slid smoothly open with hardly a murmur at her floor.

Mark stepped out with her. She supposed he must live on this floor too, and felt compelled to ask.

'No,' he said, 'I'm on the floor above.'

His nearness unnerved her so that she fumbled in her bag for the key and spilled most of the contents out on to the floor. Without a word, Mark retrieved them, handed them back, but retained the key. He opened the door and was about to follow her in when she turned and said,

'Thanks for your help.' Her expression was withdrawn. 'I'll be all right now.'

It was obvious that she did not want him near her,

so he turned away. Claire was about to close the front door when she recalled the words that had precipitated her faint. 'Just a minute!' she called after him.

He swung round. Her face, which had been drained of colour was now pink. Her eyes, which had looked at him with barely concealed loathing, were bright with anger.

'What did you mean by accusing me of being a disgrace to the nursing profession? You don't even know me!'

Mark walked back towards her. As he approached her her fists tightened. She had to do something to prevent herself from running inside and bolting the door, for the face which looked at her had the same expression on it as the face in her dream. It was only her professional pride, stronger than her fear, that prevented her.

Mark stopped when he was a foot away. 'I don't need to know you to form that opinion.' Disdain thickened his voice and his eyes narrowed. 'I saw the horror on your face when you looked at my companion's disfigurement.' His lips curled in disgust. 'It's bad enough for Susie when the general public stare, but for a staff nurse to show her feelings. . .' He shook his head. 'That's unforgivable.'

Claire's pale face became grey and she had to grip the door's edge to prevent herself staggering. How could she tell him the truth? How could she tell him that he had caused her expression of horror, and not his companion's disfigurement? He was the consultant on her ward, and unless he asked for her to be relieved from duty over this she would have to work with him. So she said nothing.

His anger at her lack of an explanation was tempered with compassion when he saw the bleakness of her expression and the wretchedness in her eyes. Something was seriously wrong with this girl. Mixed with his compassion was a desire to pull her into his arms, to kiss her misery away, to make passionate love to her. It disconcerted him that this slip of a woman who was more like a girl should affect him so, but his face showed nothing of his thoughts. His eyes were as bleak as hers, and Claire supposed their expression was due to the disdain he was feeling, which was partly true.

'I see that my impression was correct,' he said when she still did not speak.

His words fell on Claire like frozen snowflakes. They were spoken with a harshness he was unable to prevent—indeed, he did not want to prevent, for it was his only defence against the compassion and desire that he felt for this stricken girl.

Claire was held to the spot. She could not move, and was compelled to watch him turn and stride towards the lift, his broad shoulders squared, his back straight. Only when he entered it was she released. Turning, she closed the door behind her.

It took all her strength to reach the bed. Stripping off her suit, she crept under the duvet in her bra and pants, welcoming its softness as it moulded itself to her body. She was so cold she felt she would never become warm again, but gradually the heat generated by the duvet penetrated her skin, although it could not reach the dead feeling inside her.

CHAPTER FOUR

WHEN Claire woke next morning and looked at her bedside clock she could not believe the finger was pointing to seven. She had slept well and had not had the dream.

She rose and stretched as she walked to the window. As she drew the curtains aside, the sun made her screw up her eyes. It was another cloudless day.

She bathed and found herself humming as she put on her uniform. She even felt hungry and fried herself some bacon and egg, something she only did on holiday.

It was only as she waited for the lift that her lightness of mood vanished. She remembered Mark Stanger's words and hoped she would not meet him in the lift. A great sigh escaped her lips when the doors opened to an empty interior.

Normally she was happy when she went to work, but today — what would Mark say? How would he react?

'We had a new admission in the night — Melanie Roberts.' The night staff nurse, Karen Smith, was giving the report. 'Apparently the child had woken and wanted a drink. She tripped on her nightie at the top of the stairs and fell down them.' Karen's shoulders sagged wearily. 'She seemed all right in Casualty and Ronnie North was going to send her home, but when he looked at the X-rays there was a hairline fracture of her skull, so she was admitted for observation.' Karen pulled the case-notes forward. 'The parents were very upset, but I managed to persuade the father to go home. Mrs Roberts stayed,' Karen brushed a loose hair from her forehead. 'I put little Melanie in the side-ward.'

'Good,' Jessica said briskly. 'Now off you go and get a good night's rest.' She patted the night nurse's shoulder.

'Check on the children, will you, Staff?' Jessie said when the night staff had left and the day staff had been delegated their duties. 'I'll go and see Melanie.'

Children's voices raised in argument greeted Claire as she walked into the ward. Twins who had had their tonsils removed and were due for discharge next day were pulling a rag doll between them.

'He's mine!' Sally Williams's face was furious.

'No, he's not — he's mine!' Andrea was equally determined.

Claire looked around the ward in the twins' vicinity and saw an identical doll hanging half in and half out of Andrea's bed. Swiftly she retrieved it.

'Look what I've found hiding in your bed, Andrea.' She held up the toy.

The six-year-old snatched it from her. 'I didn't say you could have a lie-in this morning,' she admonished the doll.

'See? Told you this one was mine.' Sally's face was triumphant.

Claire continued on her way. She had almost finished checking the children when one of the more precocious of them said, 'Mandy's pulling off her dressing, Staff.'

'Thank you, Linda,' said Claire, hurrying over to a child of four who was sitting up in bed picking at the dressing covering her repair of inguinal hernia.

'I don't think we should take that off just yet,' Claire said in a soothing voice, smiling down at the worried face raised to hers.

'But it itches,' was the plaintive reply, as Claire pressed the tapes into place.

Tears welled in the child's blue eyes and the pretty

face reddened with the effort she was making not to cry.

Claire sat on the bed and lifted the child on to her knee. 'It's all right to cry, darling,' she said.

Warm tears soaked through her uniform as Mandy said,

'D-Daddy said I could have a new doll if I didn't cry.'

Claire tipped the small face so that Mandy could see her. 'You've been a very good girl, and we won't tell him you cried.' She smiled cheerfully at the child, whose face brightened. 'But I'm sure he wouldn't mind.'

Claire loved the feel of the young body in her arms and longed for the day when she would hold her own child. Her eyes saddened as she wondered if she ever would.

She lifted the little girl down and sat her on a small chair. Footsteps clacking on the wooden floor drew Claire's eyes. Mandy's mother was approaching with a large doll in her arms, and Mandy's eyes lit with excitement.

'Mummy, Mummy!' she cried, holding out her arms and opening and closing her fists.

Claire smiled and left them. In the office, Claire did not immediately see Mark. He was standing with his back towards her, staring out of the window.

Jessie looked up from the Kardex, and Claire was relieved to see a smile on her face. Mark could not have said anything about his opinion of her, she thought.

'Mr Stanger needs a trained children's nurse to assist him,' Jessie smiled. 'So I volunteered you.' She glanced towards Mark's back. 'I'll let him explain.'

Claire's misery deepened. She did not even think of Mark as the man in her dream. He was a doctor who scorned her as a professional, and she was amazed that he had accepted Jessie's offer of her services. Then she recalled how Jessie had told her that apart from herself Claire was the only other sick children's trained nurse on the ward. The rest of the staff were SENs or auxiliaries.

Mark turned from the window. He was so tall and broad she felt dwarfed at five foot five. He must be over six foot.

'I'll fill you in as we go,' he said, his face unsmiling as he opened the door for her to precede him.

Claire had to walk quickly to keep up with his long stride. He was wearing a dark pinstriped suit, white shirt and black and red patterned tie. He looked very distinguished, and she felt the pull of him, the attraction she would deny.

She glanced up at his angular face and felt the desire she would suppress rise and rise, making her blush. Glass doors ran the length of the corridor. The sun shone the whole length of the floor, casting their shadows sideways so that their silhouettes seemed to be chasing them.

'We're visiting a child whose parents have been against him being admitted to hospital.'

Mark stopped suddenly so that Claire, a step or two in front, had to turn and face him.

The bright light painted her face with a delicate glow, giving it a colour it did not have. The pinched look he had noted in her features as they walked together had gone, and it was a fragile face that looked up at him, more so because of her fair skin and blonde hair. Mark had a sudden urge to touch it, but was afraid that if he did she might disappear like gossamer.

He frowned at his fancifulness. If ever there was a man with his feet on the ground it was Mark.

'This child, Tommy Harper, should have been admitted to hospital some time ago, but his parents refused.' He sighed. 'Apparently the child was handled badly when he was in hospital at three years old.' He waved his hand sideways. An inexperienced nurse told him that if he didn't eat his meals the doctor wouldn't let him go home.' Mark gave Claire a thoughtful look, and she guessed he was wondering what her approach to the child would be.

This was too much. She might not have been able to explain her position where his companion was concerned, but she was not going to let him suppose she was heartless.

'I can assure you I always tell the truth to my small patients and treat them with the utmost care.' The words were spoken quietly and did not betray the anger she was feeling. Her eyes did not slide from his, and the proud carriage of her head gave her a dignity beyond her years.

'Hmm,' he murmured to cover the surge of feeling the sight of her evoked.

He took hold of her arm, and the touch of her flesh was soft beneath his fingers, causing his heart to beat faster and that treacherous desire he thought he had suppressed rose once more to torment him.

Her resentment at his taking hold of her in such a peremptory manner made her forget how she had flinched when she had seen Sammy kiss the surgeon's cheek.

'Tommy has a coarctation of the aorta.' He glanced down at her. 'You do know what that is?' He raised an enquiring eyebrow.

Claire pulled her arm away. 'Of course,' she said crossly, no longer able to hide her anger, but this anger was not only directed at him, it was also herself she was furious with. His touch had aroused, not feelings of revulsion, but a longing, a yearning to be held in his arms. It was sudden, and confused her. How could the only man who attracted her sexually be the double of the man in her dream?

It took a supreme effort for her to answer him

evenly, but she managed it, and said, 'Of course I know what a coarctation of the aorta is. It's a narrowing of the aorta, the longest artery in the body.'

Mark clapped his hands. 'Very good.' His eyes were amused. 'Tell me more.'

Claire searched his face for signs of mockery, but finding none, continued, 'There's a narrowing near to the start of the left subclavian artery, causing the flow of blood to be obstructed in the aorta, increasing the pressure in the left ventricle.

Mark grinned. He was delighted that Claire had lost that fearful look which passed fleetingly across her face whenever she had to confront him.

Claire smiled in return, cheered that he was pleased with her.

'I see you know your stuff,' he said as they stepped out of the hospital and crossed to his car. Opening the passenger door, he held it while she settled into her seat. As he joined her on his side he said, 'Now tell me what symptoms present in the patient.' The powerful Rover engine purred as he switched on the ignition.

'In a child, they grow and develop normally, but may have leg cramps, headaches and feel tired. One of the complications, though, is congestive cardiac failure.'

'Good.' He smiled sideways at her. 'This little chap. . .' he paused to turn left out of the hospital gates. 'I wanted to admit for elective surgery last year before he presented with congestive symptoms, but the parents refused, for the reasons I've mentioned already.' Mark frowned more in sadness than irritation.

They were driving beside the park. Mark drew up outside their block of flats, and Claire presumed that this was where their patient lived. Turning off the engine, he turned to her and said, 'I'll wait while you change.'

Then she understood. Tommy would be less frightened if she wasn't in uniform.

In her flat, she slipped on a beige skirt in a soft material, a sleeveless white cotton blouse, and slid her feet into brown flatties. Snatching up a white cardigan and brown shoulder bag, she was back in the car within five minutes, and was pleased to see Mark's smile of approval.

They drove to the end of the park and turned left, away from the green trees and flowerbeds bright with red geraniums.

When the car stopped at the traffic-lights at Summerton Roade, Mark glanced at her and said, 'Tommy's condition has deteriorated, and his parents are frantic. They've begged me to operate, so I've arranged for a private ambulance to take him to London, but it's essential for him to arrive in a calm condition.'

The traffic-lights changed to green. As they moved away Mark said, 'The ambulance will be equipped with everything we should need.'

Claire was surprised. A consultant did not usually travel with a patient.

'I have a particular interest in this patient,' Mark explained. It was as if he had read her thoughts. 'This will be the first time I've performed this operation.'

All the softening she had felt towards him hardened at his words. He appeared like the man in her dream — tough, uncompromising. His only interest was in performing the operation — in furthering his experience. He wasn't thinking of the child.

Mark saw the change in her, how her hands clenched, how her face tightened, and realised how his words must have sounded. He was too proud to explain that he had followed Tommy's case from babyhood and so had a special interest in the little boy.

Her supposition that he was the unfeeling one, when he had seen evidence of her lack of compassion for Susie, aggravated him into saying,

'I hope you're not going to let Tommy down,' putting into words his doubts about her.

Anger flashed in her eyes. What right had he to speak to her like that when he had spoken so callously about Tommy?

'I can assure you that it won't be *me* who lets Tommy down.' The blue eyes looked at him with distaste.

The gears crashed as he lowered to third to overtake a car, and this annoyed him further. He was behaving like a teenager, letting this young woman affect him so.

The rest of the journey was completed in silence, both of them aware of the other to a degree that was uncomfortable. Attraction, desire and anger seemed to thicken the atmosphere in the car, so that Claire felt stifled.

Shortly afterwards they turned into the drive of a large Victorian house. A small ambulance was parked outside, and a middle-aged man in uniform climbed from the driver's seat as they drew up beside him.

Mark left Claire to step from the car while he spoke to the ambulanceman. 'I think it would be better if you wait here for now,' he said. The man nodded and climbed back into his seat.

Mark signalled for Claire to follow him. The front door opened as they reached it and a man of about forty-five greeted them.

'This is Miss Forrest,' Mark introduced Claire with a wave of his hand. 'She's a trained children's nurse.'

The anxious look on Mr Harper's face deepened, but he made no comment. Claire smiled, and the gentleness of her smile, the delicacy of her face and the Alice-in-Wonderland quality about her seemed to reassure Mr Harper so that he smiled tentatively back.

Mark too was reassured. Perhaps Jessie had been right. Perhaps this young woman who so disturbed him was a gifted children's nurse.

They followed Mr Harper upstairs. The carpet sank beneath Claire's feet. Its quality was superb and the red and brown colours in its pattern blended perfectly to create a muted warmth.

Mr Harper opened a door on the right at the end of the landing, its oiled hinges making no noise. The room was decorated in colours of blue — light walls, darker ceiling. The duvet on the child's bed had Superman blazened across its front. The child looked even smaller beneath the huge figure.

A woman in her late thirties was sitting beside the bed. She raised an anxious face as her husband approached with Claire and Mark. A storybook fell from her knees as she rose, her hands clasped nervously together.

Her anxiety was transmitted to Tommy. He drew his eyebrows together as he looked up at Claire — the stranger.

Claire smiled lovingly at the frail child, and this seemed to convince Tommy that she did not pose a threat, for the worry lines left his face and he smiled back.

Mark was delighted at this sign of a rapport between patient and nurse and envied Claire her ability to communicate so effectively with Tommy. He was also grateful, for it would make it easier for him.

Claire knelt beside the bed and said, 'Hello, Tommy.'

The sick child stretched out his hand towards her and she took it in both her own, hiding her concern at how transparent the small face was and how blue the small lips were. His breathing was becoming laboured. A cylinder of oxygen was beside the bed, close to where she was kneeling. Rising, she took the small mask and, glancing towards the mother for permission and receiving a nod, she placed the mask very slowly on to the child's face, saying,

'How about taking a little puff of this? It'll help you to breathe more easily.' Her tone was as gentle as her face.

Mark watched in astonishment as Tommy allowed Claire to slip the band behind his head and position the mask.

'Tommy doesn't like the mask!' Betty Harper's tone was sharp with hostility. She had expected her son to object.

Claire saw Betty Harper's resentment at her success and explained, 'It's just because I'm new and he's intrigued.'

She glanced down at Tommy and was concerned to see the anxiety in his eyes. His mother's words had upset him, and he raised a hand to pull off the mask, but Claire took it before he could do so and held his hand in both of her own. It was such a cold little hand that it touched her heart, and she could feel tears near the surface, but controlled them.

Mark sat down on the other side of the bed close to Betty. 'Well, Tommy,' his tone was cheerful, 'how would you like a ride in an ambulance?' He made it sound like an adventure.

Tommy's eyes brightened.

'But must he go?' Betty asked plaintively.

Mr Harper took his wife's arm and led her away from the bed. 'You know he must,' he murmured in a low voice.

'But I can stay with him?' The hazel eyes, so like her son's, filled with tears.

'Of course.' Mark's voice broke the tension. It was so full of confidence that even Claire felt better.

Swiftly Mark took the oxygen mask from the frail face, wrapped Tommy in the duvet and moved towards the door, all this accomplished with a gentleness that surprised Claire.

Mark's expression was one of irritation as he looked

at her. 'The door,' was the peremptory command, and she hurried to open it.

They were soon in the ambulance. Mark switched on the oxygen and was about to lower the mask when Tommy looked appealingly at Claire. He was too ill to speak.

Mark made way for her in the confined space. She brushed against him as she passed, and was disturbed at how her awareness of him flared at this small contact. Bizarre or not, there was no doubt about it — she was attracted to this man. She took the mask from him with a hand that trembled slightly and hoped he would think the reason for her nervousness was her concern for Tommy. She did not want to look at Mark, but felt compelled to, and blushed when she saw his amused smile.

Quickly she slipped the strap behind the boy's head and concentrated on making him more comfortable. She tried to forget Mark's presence, but the doctor seemed to fill the ambulance.

There was not enough room inside for the parents to travel with them. Claire had felt Betty's resentment as the mother watched her climb in with Tommy and Mark. She heard Betty Harper say, 'I should be the one to go with him, not that nurse. I'm his mother,' in a complaining voice, but did not hear Mr Harper's reply. She did see them take their seats in his car, preparing to follow.

Claire thought Tommy might be agitated without his mother, but he seemed calmer. She stroked the brown hair from his forehead and held the cold hand, but did not speak. Eventually he closed his eyes and slept.

When the ambulance swung round the corner too quickly and she was thrown against Mark she felt a shiver of excitement and bent over Tommy so that Mark would not see her agitation, but a sudden vision of a miniature Mark superimposing itself over Tommy's features unnerved her further, so that she was glad when the hospital was reached.

There was no sign of Tommy's parents when the ambulance doors opened. 'They must have been held up by traffic,' said Mark.

So it was Claire who accompanied the child on the trolley to the ward. Mark had gone straight to Theatre.

'Are you the mother?' The ward sister in charge of the children's ward met them.

'No,' Claire said shortly. 'Don't you recognise me, Sister Bennett?'

Moira Bennett frowned, then her face cleared.

'Nurse Forrest, isn't it?' She smiled. Claire had been one of her favourite students. 'I didn't recognise you out of uniform.'

'Tommy's parents are following by car,' Claire explained. 'They should be here soon.'

Moira looked past Claire. 'Mr Stanger. . .?'

'Went straight to Theatre.'

'Ah, yes.' Moira smiled down at Tommy, who turned his head away, his small hand tightening on Claire's, his face frightened, his breathing more laboured.

'Don't worry, sweetheart,' she said gently. 'I'm here.'

His face relaxed. Claire helped Moira transfer the small boy to a bed in the side-ward. At the door, the ward sister said,

'Tommy hasn't had anything to eat or drink, has he?' Her eyes were anxious.

'No,' Claire hastened to reassure her.

'Are you to stay?'

As Mark had not said, Claire did not know. She only knew that she could not leave Tommy until he was in Theatre and his mother had arrived.

'I'll stay for the time being,' she said, and explained how frightened of hospital her small patient was.

'Yes,' said Moira, 'Mr Stanger told me. Tommy's a

special patient of his. He's looked after the boy since he was first admitted some time ago.' She glanced towards the fragile child. 'He seems to have confidence in you, though, so I think it would be important if you were to special him now and when he returns. I'll speak to Mr Stanger about it.'

'But I'm not intensive-care trained,' Claire pointed out, feeling awful about misjudging Mark concerning Tommy.

'That doesn't matter,' Moira told her. 'The specialised staff will be there. You'll just give him confidence.'

'Right.' Though Claire couldn't help feeling nervous.

The anaesthetist came, and was very gentle with Tommy. Dr Robinson was a big bear-like man whom the children adored, but whom Claire disliked. He had cornered her in this ward's treatment-room when she was taking her children's certificate and tried to kiss her. Her slap had not been well received, but he gave no sign of recognising her now, and for this she was grateful.

Half an hour later Tommy was due to go to Theatre, and his parents had still not arrived.

'You'll have to go with the boy, Claire,' said Moira. 'I'll tell the parents when they arrive.' She handed over the case-notes. 'It's a good job the consent form's been signed.'

As Claire agreed she felt a shiver, and wondered why, but the thought left her mind as she concentrated on keeping Tommy calm, holding his hand all the way to Theatre. He was almost asleep when they arrived at the anaesthetic-room.

'Pleased to see your patient so peaceful, Staff?' There was a sardonic look in James Robinson's eyes. He *had* recognised Claire.

'I can't take all the credit for that,' Claire said wryly. 'The pre-op you prescribed helped.'

'I would really like to operate today.' Mark's dry

voice came from the door to the scrub-room. He wore theatre green trousers and was stripped to the waist. His chest did not look as broad as it did in a jacket. A light tan from his sail the other day made his skin appear smooth and silky, and Claire had a sudden desire to touch it, to feel its texture. Her breathing quickened as she fought to suppress this feeling, her face colouring with the effort, for it was more important that James Robinson should not suspect how Mark was affecting her than for the consultant to see the gleam of awareness in her eyes.

'Am I to return to Whiteleigh?' she asked Mark, and was appalled to hear how husky her voice sounded.

Mark did not seem to notice, for he answered sharply, 'No. Surely you realise that you'll have to be here when Tommy comes round?' His long stride brought him close to her, and she could see how the hair on his chest curled.

James Robinson had intubated Tommy by now, and Claire could feel the anaesthetist's eyes watching Mark and herself.

'The boy has confidence in you, and that's of prime importance.' Mark sounded as if he did not reciprocate that confidence. 'You'd better go back to the ward and wait.' It was an order.

Claire was cross. She could not understand why what to her was a reasonable question should have been received with such annoyance. She was not going to let him dismiss her as if she was a student nurse, so she said, 'Yes, sir,' so coolly that it was offensive, and she saw Mark's fists clench, but he did not reply, just swung away back into the scrub-room.

'So-oo!' The anaesthetist's voice cut through Claire's aggravation, its sly tone immediately alerting her.

She turned swiftly, her skirt swishing against the anaesthetic machine, and looked at him as coldly as she had looked at Mark.

'So?' She raised her eyebrows.

But James was not abashed. 'So you're not as frigid as I thought.'

Claire was livid, and more so because he had voiced her fears. 'You really are a bastard!' she snapped surprising herself.

The use of the word coming from someone he had always thought such a prude shocked James into silence.

The theatre staff came in to take Tommy, and Claire returned to the ward, more aggravated by James's insinuations than by Mark's behaviour.

Her face was still set in annoyed lines when she reached the ward and met Betty Harper coming out of the sister's office.

'No doubt you're looking like that because I'm here,' she accused Claire, her face angry. 'Why are you trying to take my little boy away from me?' she demanded.

Ian Harper had hold of his wife's arm and was trying to pull her closer to his side.

Claire was astounded and for a moment speechless. Then she darted forward, her hand outstretched.

'You're wrong,' she blurted out in agitation, and realised as soon as she had spoken how Betty could misconstrue her words, and this was exactly what the distraught mother did.

'Are you implying that I'm the wrong mother for my son?' Betty was incensed.

Moira Bennett rushed out of the office. 'Please, please,' she implored. 'You'll upset the children.' She looked at Ian Harper. 'Bring your wife in here, Mr Harper.' She opened the door to the side-ward which Tommy had vacated.

Betty Harper was in tears and leaned heavily on her husband's arm. Claire was very upset. She had never been accused like that before and did not know how to deal with Betty's jealousy.

In the side-ward, Moira Bennett said, 'Sit down, Mrs Harper,' in a firm voice. Betty took the chair her husband pushed forward. 'Your behaviour just now is not going to help your son,' Moira said in a not ungentle voice. 'Staff Nurse Forrest understands that the anxiety and stress you're under made you speak that way.' Betty Harper was crying quietly, and Claire reached for a tissue in the box beside the bed and handed it to her. Betty took it from her without looking up.

'Quite often children will obey a stranger where they won't their parents,' Moira said. She placed a hand on the weeping woman's shoulder. 'Nurse Forrest isn't trying to take Tommy from you. She wants to help make him better, and it's fortunate that he likes her, because she's going to look after him when he returns from Theatre.'

Betty looked up, her eyes drier, her expression weary. She seemed older, and Claire forgot her own distress when she saw how worn Tommy's mother was.

'Please forgive me, Claire,' Betty whispered. Claire was touched that she had remembered her name. 'I don't know why I behaved so.'

'You're just tired,' said Claire gently. Her tone was resonant yet soft, almost hypnotic. It seemed to calm Betty. 'Why don't you have a lie-down? Sister will let you know when Tommy returns to Intensive Care.'

'I most certainly will,' Moira endorsed Claire's offer. 'You can use this room, and I'll ask a nurse to bring you some tea.'

'Thanks.' Betty's voice was low, but she managed a smile.

'You handled Mrs Harper very well,' said Moira when they were back in the office. 'Have you ever thought of becoming a ward sister?'

Claire had been undecided about her future career; that was why she had taken an agency job. Somehow she could not see herself in a sister's uniform, so she said, 'I don't think I have enough experience yet.'

'Perhaps you do need a little longer to think about it,' Moira smiled. 'But we need people like you.'

Claire was flattered and her normally serious face broke into a smile of pleasure. 'Thanks for the compliment, Sister.'

'You'd better go to the intensive-care unit and introduce yourself,' said Moira, then she frowned as she looked at Claire's plain clothes. 'It's a pity you're not in uniform.'

Claire explained Mark's reason for her mode of dress, and Moira's frown deepened. 'I think you'll have to put some sort of covering over your clothes, though.' Then her face brightened. 'Run up to Theatre and borrow a gown.'

Claire doubted if that was a good idea, but she didn't say so. She went to one of the theatres which was nearing the end of its cases. Moira had told her to ask for Sister Michaels.

'Just put it in the ward bin when you've finished with it,' the dark-haired sister said when Claire had explained her reason for wanting the gown.

Claire was waiting in Intensive Care when Tommy was brought down. The little boy was very pale, almost lifeless, and she could not help but be anxious when she saw him attached to a ventilator and heart monitor. She was not used to such high-powered and specialised equipment, and was glad that she would not have total responsibility for Tommy. The specially trained staff were there for that. The sister in charge of the unit came and showed Claire how they liked their recordings charted and left Claire reading Tommy's case-notes.

Half an hour later, Claire had just recorded her observations and was putting the top on her pen, when Mark appeared at her side.

'What are you wearing that gown for?' he whispered fiercely. 'I don't want Tommy seeing you in it.'

Claire was tired. She was worried about Tommy even though his vital signs were normal, and Betty Harper's attack had left her drained. She turned towards Mark, who was not in theatre greens, but was wearing the suit he had left Whiteleigh in. His black hair was still wet from his shower and clung to his head, sleek like an advertisement for haircream. The lines of his face had deepened with fatigue and his shoulders were not as square as usual. It was as if the operation had drained his energy and shrunk his body. His clothes hung on him loosely.

Claire's anger dissolved, and compassion for the exhausted, worried surgeon took its place. The strain he was feeling was much greater than hers. This was the first time he had performed an anastomosis of the aorta. So she said quietly.

'Sister Bennett thought it advisable.'

Her eyes were very gentle. He had seen her look at Tommy like that, and he was suddenly furious. He did not want her to look at him as if he was a child. He wanted. . . What did he want? Then it came to him. He wanted to crush her in his arms, kiss her until she was breathless. He wanted to make glorious, passionate love to her. His face flushed with his effort to control the fever of his desire. But he knew he would have to be especially careful with her, for the fear of him, shown on occasions, seemed to go deeper than was warranted by her virginal state.

'Well, take it off.' His voice was gruff.

'Yes, sir,' Claire said stiffly, pulling at the tapes behind her neck with such vehemence that they broke.

Mark was studying the charts. 'Has his mother seen him yet?'

'No.'

'I don't want her to see him at the moment.' He kept his eyes on the notes. 'It would upset her.'

'Are you sure?' Claire thought Tommy's mother would want to reassure herself that her son was really back from Theatre, even though he was attached to machines and would be sedated until tomorrow.

Mark's black brows drew together and his expression was fierce as he said, 'Are you questioning my judgement?'

Claire felt the old tremor, the tremor associated with the man in her dream, but she pushed it aside and found the courage to answer, 'Yes,' and was amazed at how bold she sounded.

Throughout her training she had always deferred to those in authority even when she felt they were wrong. But now, perhaps because the man in her dream was no longer a nebulous figure, lack of confidence in herself had been swept away.

'Mrs Harper has been under considerable strain. I'm sure that knowing Tommy's operation has been a success will release her from this and she'll be able to look at Tommy with calmness, providing she's prepared for all this beforehand.' Claire gestured at the tubes and machines. 'It will be good for Tommy to see his mum when he wakes up tomorrow, for, no matter how much he likes me, he loves her.'

Mark's anger left him. She was right. His expression was one of amusement as he said, 'Thanks for the vote of confidence.' Then his face straightened and he sighed. 'I just hope it isn't misplaced.'

Claire heard the vulnerability beneath his words, a vulnerability the man in her dream never had, and she placed a hand on his arm. The cloth was smooth to the touch and she could feel the strength of his forearm beneath the material.

Glancing up into his face, she saw, not the mature man she was half afraid of, but the serious surgeon who had doubts in spite of his experience, and she knew she would never be afraid of him again.

She smiled openly, the first time she had done so, and the friction between them disappeared. They both felt it. Claire found she could look at Mark with friendship, the same friendship she had for Steven. Mark, sensing a change in her, knew he must not take advantge of this softening towards him, but it didn't still the desire that heated his body.

'I'll send someone to fetch Tommy's mother,' he said, and touched her fleetingly on the shoulder before he left.

Claire could still feel where his fingers had brushed her shoulder when Betty Harper was brought to the bedside.

'Mr Stanger told me what to expect when I saw Tommy, but it's still a shock.' A small sob escaped her lips.

Claire put an arm round her. 'He'll be fine,' she said with confidence, and smiled at Ian Harper, who was standing helplessly at the foot of the bed. She drew him forward and placed chairs so that the couple could sit close to their son.

Throughout the day mother and father came and went quietly, like shadows, keeping out the nurses' way and deferring to them whenever needed.

When Tommy opened his eyes next day and saw his mother, his smile touched Claire's heart, and she wished it had been for her. It was then that she faced up to how lonely she was and had been for years. Even the closeness between Steven and herself was threatened by his awareness of her as a woman and not his childhood 'pet'.

Claire stayed at the children's hospital for a further three days. Tommy's mother beside him reassured the boy more than Claire could, and now that the operation was over Betty was no longer apprehensive, and her calmness soothed Tommy. He had accepted the staff on the unit, so Claire was redundant, but she was reluctant to go. She knew she should not become emotionally involved with her small patients, but she could not help it; they filled a need in her. And it had been enough until now. This time it was different. Claire envied Betty Harper and was jealous of Tommy's love for his mother. Their positions had reversed. The wall Claire had built around her emotions had cracked.

Her relationship with the other nurses on the unit had changed as well. The reserve she had approached her colleagues with during her children's training had left her.

'If you're staying,' Jill, one of the nurses on the intensive-care unit, had said when Claire arrived, 'I can lend you a nightie.'

'Thanks.' Claire had been glad to accept the offer.

Jill had looked thoughtfully at the girl she had trained with. 'You don't wish you'd stayed here and specialised?'

In the past, Claire would have evaded the question with a smile, but now she said, 'Not really. I like it in Whiteleigh.'

'And the gorgeous Mr Stanger goes there quite a bit.' Jill's smile was not sly, it was wistful.

Claire would have given Jill a cool look a few weeks ago, but today she just smiled and said, 'Yes.'

Mark phoned the nurses' home the evening before Claire was due to return to Whiteleigh. 'I'm going down myself tomorrow, so I can give you a lift,' he offered.

'Thanks,' she accepted easily, 'I'd appreciate it.'

There was a pause, then Mark asked, 'Are you doing anything this evening?' It was six o'clock.

'I had thought of visiting a friend,' said Claire.

'If it's not definite, I'll pick you up at seven-thirty

and take you out for a meal.' Before she could refuse he added, 'It's by way of a thank-you for your care of Tommy.'

Claire did not know if she was ready, yet, to see Mark in any other way than professionally, but the food in the hospital canteen could be better and she was hungry, so she accepted.

It was a nervous Claire who replaced the receiver. She hadn't anything to wear apart from what she had travelled to London in and a blouse Jill had lent her; it was white with long sleeves and very plain, but it would have to do. She just hoped Mark would not take her anywhere sophisticated.

When he called for her, his fawn trousers and white designer jacket with a casual shirt of the same colour reassured her.

'I thought we'd go into the country,' he said. 'It's a lovely evening.' He was looking more rested.

'I'd like that.' Claire smiled tentatively.

He led her to a red sports car parked at the kerb.

'A friend who's away has lent it to me for a while,' he explained. 'Said I wanted to impress my girlfriend,' and he winked.

This made her laugh and she relaxed, as he had meant her to.

As she took her seat beside him, Steven came into her mind. His car was identical except the colour.

The evening was warm and clammy, but as they drove out of London in the direction of Richmond and left the tall buildings behind, the air became cooler, fresher. A slight breeze lifted her fringe.

She glanced at Mark's profile as he concentrated on the traffic. There was strength in the line of his jaw, yet gentleness in the curve of his lips. They suddenly smiled as if he knew she was assessing him, and she blushed.

'Not such an ogre, then?'

'An ogre?' She threw the word back at him to give herself time to think. The word had flashed the man in her dream before her eyes. Mark was too near the truth.

'Yes.' Mark's tone was light, little realising what his choice of words had conjured up. 'I've felt sometimes that you're afraid of me, though I can't think why.'

'It must be your driving,' Claire quipped, pleased with her inspiration.

He laughed and let it pass, as he was negotiating a difficult piece in the narrow road.

A silence fell between them, one Claire did not know how to break. Mark's nearness was disconcerting and she was beginning to wish she had not accepted his invitation. A mundane meal in the hospital cafeteria was preferable to this tension.

'We'll soon be there now.' Mark had not appeared to notice her quietness, and she relaxed.

She would liked to have told him that she wasn't afraid of him and that she looked on him as a friend, but then she might have to explain her previous coldness.

Mark turned into a narrow leafy road, the sun casting patterns across his face. 'Do you come from Whiteleigh?'

His sudden question ruffled her for a moment. Then she answered, 'No, Surrey. My uncle and aunt brought me up when my mother died.' She gave him the information diffidently and he had the impression that she did not want to continue with this line of conversation, but he persisted. How else could he help her if he did not know anything about her background? For it was in this background that he intuitively felt lay the answer to her trouble, and troubled she was.

'You must miss them,' he commented.

'Yes, I do. They're away at the moment. My uncle's an architect and he's been invited to lecture at a university in California.' She wondered if she would have told her aunt about Mark; she certainly hadn't written about him. She knew Steven would not have told his mother about Mark's similarity to the man in her dream. Her aunt thought Claire had stopped having the nightmare, and Claire had made Steven promise not to delude her.

Her thoughts were distracted as Mark turned into the car park of a pub set back from the road. It was peaceful here, and Claire took a deep breath of clean air as she stepped from the car.

When Mark took her arm and led her past the pub, she glanced up at him in surprise, but her surprise turned to horror when she saw a houseboat tied up beside the river at the back of the pub. It was obviously being used as a restaurant, and Mark was leading her to it.

The smile left Mark's face when he saw her stricken expression. He had hoped to please her with the originality of his choice. He wanted her to relax in his company, he wanted to break down the barrier he sensed was between them. He felt she had accepted him to some extent, but now. . .

'I can't go on that boat!' Claire cried, backing away, her hand fluttering in a rejecting gesture, her eyes round with dread. Pictures she had suppressed suddenly rose before her eyes, her face became deathly pale and she sank to the ground in a faint.

When she regained consciousness, the face she saw bending over her was the face of the man in her dream, and she could not speak, her fear was so great. This time it was real. The whiteness was there, the intentness of the eyes, and she was cold, just as she was in the nightmare. No, this was real—real—panic opened her mouth in a scream, but no sound came, and she felt her skin shrivel with horror.

'Claire!'

A warm hand touched her face, but she shrank away, still locked in the dream.

'Claire!' Mark raised his voice, its firmness concealing his concern. 'There's nothing to be afraid of. If you don't want to go on the houseboat we can eat in the pub,' and he smiled.

It was his smile, gentle and sincere, more than his mundane words that snapped her out of her nightmare. This man was not in her dream. This was Mark — alive, smiling.

'Mark,' she whispered, and did not realise it was the first time she had used his Christian name, she was so relieved to find he was real.

She clutched at his sleeve, and it was then that she saw its colour — white, and started to tremble.

'Claire!' He frowned. 'What is it?'

Again the softness of his voice calmed her. 'Oh, Mark!' It was a cry for help.

Her troubled face tore at his heart. He was sitting on the bed and he caught her into his arms, holding her gently against him, and stroked her hair.

'There now, all will be well,' he murmured, the feel of her against him soothing his yearning, yet at the same time sending his desire soaring.

Claire looked up into his face, and all the confusion she had felt where he was concerned fell away. He had rescued her from the dream and she was grateful, but she could not tell him what was troubling her.

When he saw her composure Mark laid her back on the pillows. Claire looked around her. 'Where are we?' She was not alarmed to find herself on a bed somehow. She trusted Mark.

It was a charming room. Chintz curtains wafted at the open window, and wallpaper of a smaller design to the material added to the freshness. The duvet and pillowcases were a pale pink. There were beams above her head, not fake ones, the originals.

'The proprietress let us use this room.' Mark grinned cheekily. 'I told her I was a doctor.'

Claire grinned back, and Mark was pleased to see the colour returning to her face.

'But tell me,' his eyes were amused, 'is it just me who makes you faint?' There was concern beneath the lightly spoken words. 'Should I be flattered that you swoon at the sight of me, or should I be. . .' he was laughing now '. . .appalled?'

The latter was so near the truth that Claire blushed. 'It's because you're so handsome, such a dreamy doctor. . .' She smiled shyly and hoped he would accept this answer without question. Then she remembered the boat, and pushed herself into a sitting position, fear in her eyes. 'We won't have to go on that houseboat, will we?'

The thoughtful look on his face changed to one of seriousness. 'No, of course not.' He studied her — the clenched hands, the brittle smile — and said, 'Are you afraid of water?'

Claire grabbed at this excuse as a man would grab at an extended hand as he fell. 'Yes.'

He did not believe her. There was more here than she was telling, but he did not press her. Perhaps when he had gained her complete confidence she would tell him, and he wanted to gain her confidence — to be her friend and eventually her lover.

He leaned forward and kissed her forehead. She could smell, not aftershave, but the scent of a good soap on his skin.

Tentatively she put her hands on his shoulders and he could feel them tremble. He wanted to take them in his own, still their fluttering, calm them as he would a frightened bird, but he did not want to do anything that would scare her away.

Sitting, he was not much taller than Claire. She studied his face, and he kept perfectly still. He wished he knew why her scrutiny was so intense. He was taken by surprise when she placed her lips gently on his, and it was as if this kiss unlocked his heart. Her lips were so soft and the kiss so fleeting that it filled him with a stronger desire than any of the passionate kisses he had been given in the past. Only his strength of will prevented him from enfolding her in an embrace which would have shown her how deeply she moved him, for he knew instinctively that her kiss had been more of an experiment than an invitation.

How was it that a lovely girl, pure of spirit, beautiful of face, had been left untouched? Mark longed to be the man who would bring this fair flower to its fruition, the man who would not taint her spiritual quality, but who would increase its power by adding the colour it lacked by gently introducing her to the mysteries of, not sex, but love.

Yes, he loved her — he admitted it. She inflamed him as no other woman had. Just to touch her roused him to a pitch he had not thought possible.

Her soft blush enchanted him, and he smiled a smile no other woman had seen. 'Do you feel like eating?' he asked. He felt like laughing hysterically. How could such simple words fall from his lips when all he wanted to do was to shower her with endearments, the more flamboyant the better?

Claire was still savouring the warm sensation in her lips left by the kiss. For a moment she looked at Mark uncomprehendingly and he had to repeat the question.

Suddenly she was hungry. 'Yes,' she smiled, 'I'm ravenous.' And Mark laughed out loud.

They ate in the Elizabethan restaurant with old beams above their heads, a large fireplace set with logs in the huge grate, and furniture which complimented the era.

Mark amused her with tales of his student days, and

Claire was able to hold her own, thanks to the veneer of sophistication that Steven had given her.

When their sweet of peaches and cream arrived, Mark said, 'It's strange that you should have lost your mother when you were three — I did as well.'

Claire's peach fell from her spoon into the dish with a plop. 'Yes, that is a coincidence,' she agreed, but the face she raised to his had lost the animation her enjoyment of the evening had given it, and had become withdrawn.

Mark could have kicked himself. He knew she did not want to discuss her mother, but he thought they had been coming on so well that he might find out more about her if he mentioned the similarity of their childhood. It was too late now, so he continued with, 'Yes. My father didn't marry again, so I was brought up by my grandmother, who lived in Whiteleigh.'

He knew he had said the right thing when he saw the strain leave Claire's face, to be replaced with a smile.

'Lucky for you,' she said. 'I love Whiteleigh. We used to spend our summer holidays there when we were children.' Her eyes reflected that time of blue skies and hot sand, of buckets and spades and ice-cream. 'I loved the donkey rides. Do they still have them?'

Mark laughed at her enthusiasm. 'Yes. I'll take you on one if you like.'

She grinned. It was the first time he had seen her truly relaxed, and he liked it and smiled.

'Chicken,' he said when she did not reply.

Claire sat up straight, a mischievous gleam in her eye. 'Not on your life. I'm game if you are.'

He laughed. 'With pleasure.' Then he added cheekily, 'And I bet my donkey will outrace yours.'

She grinned. 'Done.'

'And the loser?' he asked, a slow smile spreading across his face. 'I think a kiss would be a good forfeit, don't you?'

Claire's smile became unsure. It wasn't his suggestion that caused it, but the way he was looking at her. His eyes were intense and she could feel his sexual potency. It scared yet excited her. No man had ever made her feel like this.

Mark's eyes narrowed. 'Chick ——'

Claire interrupted him. 'No way,' she said, and put out her hand for him to shake.

He took it in his own. It was slender and delicately boned, lost in his square, strong surgeon's hand, and again he was caught up in an emotion that left him speechless.

Claire blushed at the expression in his eyes, and it was this colouring of her skin that restored his voice.

'Coffee?' he asked.

'Please.'

They had their coffee outside beneath a red and white striped umbrella. The evening was still pleasant enough not to require jackets.

Their drive back was companionable. 'Does your grandmother live near the park in Whiteleigh?' Claire asked.

'She died five years ago.' Mark's tone held regret.

'I'm sorry.'

Mark glanced sideways and saw his sadness reflected on her face.

'My father died six months ago, that's why I came to Whiteleigh.' She brushed her fringe away from her forehead. 'I wanted a change.'

She did not tell him that her father's death had left her restless or that she was trying to escape from Steven's unwelcome advances.

Mark did not reply. He had to concentrate on the traffic, which was still heavy even though it was ten-thirty.

Drawing up outside the nurses' home, he said, 'I'll pick you up at eight. I'm operating at ten — Bill

Johnson's cleft palate. He's been in a week now and is used to the ward staff, who've been instructing his mother in the use of the restraints.'

Claire nodded. He had put the hood up on the sports car for the drive back. The daylight was closing and dusk darkened the car's interior and softened her outline. It almost seemed to him as if she was fading from his sight, as if she was a ghost, that he was imagining her. He reached forward, suddenly afraid.

'Claire.' His voice was urgent.

Startled, she answered, 'Yes?' and grasped the hand stretching towards her, aware of his need but not understanding it.

His hand tightened on hers and it was a moment before he replied. He had to recover from his fright.

The enclosed darkness was suffocating, and she was finding it difficult to breathe until she admitted to herself that it wasn't the confined space and the dusk that was causing her shortness of breath. It was Mark Stanger's nearness and the tension that had sprung up between them.

Then he released her hand, and she wished he hadn't. She thought she heard him sigh. Then he said,

'It was nothing,' and put his hands on the wheel.

It felt to Claire like a dismissive gesture. Her hand fumbled for the door catch. Suddenly it swung wide, almost toppling her out as she found it. Only his reaching for her saved her.

'I'll be ready at eight,' she promised as she closed the door after her.

As the car moved away, its red colour brightening the street, she could still feel his touch on her arm.

She sighed. His going had left an emptiness inside her that she knew Steven could never fill.

CHAPTER FIVE

CLAIRE reported at one o'clock next day. She had the late duty.

'You're looking pale,' Jessie Watson commented. 'London air doesn't seem to have done you any good. You must get out on the beach, get some suntan.' She smiled at her serious staff nurse. 'I'm glad you're back. Billy's due back from Theatre any minute and I'd like you to stay with him for a bit.' She yawned, and Claire thought how tired she looked. 'I've been up half the night with my husband—he had an asthmatic attack,' she explained.

'Is there anything I can do?' asked Claire, concerned. 'Would you like me to stand in for you?'

Jessie smiled. 'No, thanks, but you're a dear for asking. Jack's all right this morning and I've packed him off to the doctor's. He'll ring me if he isn't well.' She fixed her cap more firmly into place, pushing a grey curl beneath it.

'I'm putting Billy in the side-ward—a bed has been made up for his mother. She's a sensible woman, older than the usual mum, nearer forty than thirty, I'd say.' A worried frown deepened the lines on Jessie's forehead. 'I hope Billy won't be upset when he sees you. I try to use a nurse a child knows after the op, but you're the only nurse capable of caring for him.

Claire smiled. 'I'll do my best.'

Jessie's face relaxed. 'I know you will, we'll just have to hope for the best.'

Claire left Jessie in the office sighing at the pile of paperwork she had to do.

Mrs Johnson was sitting by the window when Claire

entered the side-ward. It overlooked the car park, and as Claire approached her she caught a glimpse of the red sports car. It recalled Mark vividly, as vividly as its colour, and she had to stop a gasp from escaping her lips.

'A fine day,' said Mrs Johnson, rising to greet her.

She was wearing beige trousers and a white blouse. A sudden vision of Mark dressed in the same colours flashed before Claire's eyes, and she had to push him right away from her thoughts before she could greet Mrs Johnson, but the feeling of him lingered.

'I'm Claire Forrest,' she said, smiling. 'The nurse who will look after your son.'

Jean Johnson was Claire's height, slim with a good figure. Her face tightened. 'I haven't seen you before,' she said, an anxious frown between her brows.

'I have met Billy,' Claire hastened to reassure Jean. She was determined that Jean should be at ease with her and not feel threatened. The episode with Tommy's mother had shaken her, so she used body language to set the other woman at ease.

She smiled and moved closer, her whole demeanour self-effacing and yet not negative. The way she carried her head denoted confidence. Her spotless white uniform with its cheerful tabard of bunny rabbits on a pink background over it, her delicate colouring and short hair all presented a picture of calm orderliness.

Claire was pleased to see Jean relax. 'Call me Jean,' the older woman requested.

'And I'm Claire.' She looked towards the cot prepared for Billy's return from Theatre. 'I know Sister will have told you about the post-operative care for your son, but would you like me to go over it again?'

'Oh, would you?' The lines of strain on Jean's face deepened.

'Have a seat.' Claire gestured towards an armchair, and when Jean obeyed her, sat down opposite.

'Billy will probably find breathing with his palate closed difficult, and this will worry him.' She nodded towards the croup tent. 'Steam will provide moisture to the lining of his mouth, which will be dry from breathing with it open—that's what the tent's for.' She paused to smile reassuringly. 'The hardest thing will be to stop him from crying, laughing or doing anything that will put pressure on his stitch line.'

She smiled again. 'We'll have to keep his mouth clean after each feed and moist. The tent will help with that. Mr Stanger will probably prescribe antibiotics to ensure against a mouth infection.'

'I see.' Jean smiled anxiously. 'I do understand.'

'Yes, I can see that.' Claire sounded encouraging. 'You've been feeding him with a cup and from the side of a spoon, and we'll continue with that.' She folded her hands in her lap. 'He'll have to be stimulated so that he doesn't become bored. Reading to him and playing tapes will help.' She grinned. 'I'm sure you'll have plenty of ideas.'

Jean's smile was tentative. 'I hope so.' Then she frowned. 'But what about the elbow restraints?'

Claire had not forgotten. She had deliberately left that for Jean to remember, thinking it would give her more confidence if she contributed to the care of Billy.

'Yes. Good thinking.'

Her praise lifted the lines of strain from Jean's face and a more relaxed expression lit her features.

'We'll have to do all we can to help him find them less restricting. It won't be easy because of his age, but it's vital that he doesn't put his fingers in his mouth.'

She had just finished speaking when the door opened and the theatre staff appeared with the patient. She hurried to help them. Jean leaned forward, every part of her wanting to help, yet knowing she would only be a hindrance. Claire flashed her a sympathetic smile.

The theatre staff were just leaving when Mark passed

them, still in his theatre greens. 'Hello, Mrs Johnson.' His smile seemed to illuminate the room, or so it appeared to Claire. 'I'm sure Staff here will be a great help to you during the next trying days.' He glanced in Claire's direction.

His presence filled her with a warm glow. Mark approached the cot and Claire joined him. Both their heads bent at the same time. They were so close that she could have kissed his cheek, and she had an insane desire to do so. She was glad Mark was testing the elbow restraints and did not see her face colour.

'He won't like these,' he said, looking at Jean with a smile. Then seeing the anxiety flare in her eyes he said cheerfully, 'But he'll get used to them, with your help.'

The door opened and an auxiliary came in. 'Phone call for you, Staff.' Her eyes were agleam with interest as she said, 'It's a man.'

Mark frowned his disapproval. 'Sister doesn't allow personal calls on duty.' He was looking straight at the auxiliary, whose face became aggrieved. She was only the messenger, and, anyway, this was the first time she had heard of such a ruling. Sister did not encourage phone calls, but she did not mind the occasional one.

The day outside had lost its brightness as clouds passed over the sun. The change of light darkened Claire's pale skin and fair hair, giving her a grey look. It was as if the misery she was now feeling had slipped out of the window and darkened the day, leaving her colourless.

Then she became concerned at how just a few cross words from Mark could have this effect, could make her feel devastated. It would not do, so she said,

'Tell the caller I'll be off at six,' and smiled at the auxiliary. 'He can phone me at home.'

Mollified, the girl said, 'Right, Staff,' and left them.

'I'd like a word with you outside.' Mark indicated the door.

'Shall I record Billy's vital signs first?' asked Claire, in a cool tone. She detected an unsureness in Mark which surprised her as he answered,

'Er — yes.' He frowned in annoyance at himself, but it looked to Claire as if she was the reason for his cross expression.

After she had made and recorded the necessary checks, she said to Jean Johnson, 'I'll be back in a minute,' smiling reassuringly, only glad that Jean had been too far away to hear Mark's remarks.

Claire preceded him from the room, her nervousness and misery at this sudden rift between them when she had thought they had been so close hidden behind a calm mask.

As soon as they were in the corridor she turned to face him, but did not speak, and for a moment nor did he. Then, pulling off his cap, he ran his fingers through his hair and said in a gruff voice,

'Who was that phoning you?'

Expecting him to tell her off for receiving the call, Claire was taken by surprise. Then the anger that lay beneath the surface and only appeared when she felt she was being taken advantage of surfaced.

'I don't think I have to answer that,' she said, her blue eyes cold.

Mark was appalled at his behaviour. He was acting like a jealous fool, but he could not help himself; he had to know. 'I think you'd better tell me,' he said in a severe tone.

Claire looked so slender and fragile that Mark was sure his bullying manner would produce a prompt and truthful reply. It had worked with medical students.

He did receive a reply, but not the one he wanted.

'There's nothing in my job description that says I have to tell my private affairs to the ward consultant.' Her face was white with anger. She gave him a disparaging look and, turning, went back into the side-ward, leaving him standing aghast, not only at her abrupt departure, but at his own behaviour. Part of him was surprised, though. There was steel behind the gentleness. Perhaps she wasn't as fragile as he had thought, and this heartened him.

The rest of the day passed uneventfully for Claire, but when she came off duty she was very tired. She was unlocking her car door when footsteps came up behind her. She swung round. It was Mark. Immediately she tensed.

'Claire.' He looked embarrassed. 'I apologise,' he said in a tight voice. 'You were right—I have no right to ask you about your private affairs.' He could not tell her that he was insanely jealous.

Claire sensed that this proud man did not apologise often, and relented. 'It was my cousin Steven,' she told him.

Mark could not bring himself to ask further, but he did raise an eyebrow, and Claire was suddenly amused. He could almost be jealous, she thought, and wished he was, though it seemed unlikely.

She smiled. 'He was that handsome man I was dining with at the Haven.' Then she wished she had not mentioned where Mark had seen Steven, for he replied stiffly,

'I remember,' and the tentative overture was lost.

Claire had forgotten how she had been unable to explain the look of horror that had crossed her face and how Mark had interpreted it that evening. All she could do now was watch helplessly as he turned sharply away.

Disconsolately, she climbed into her Mini and sat for a moment with her hands on the wheel. Then she sighed and gave a shrug.

'Ah, well,' she said aloud, 'I suppose I'll be able to explain one of these days.' There wasn't anything she could do about it now, so she turned on the engine, put the car into gear and moved away.

The red sports car was parked beside the Rover when she arrived at the flats. She had just left her Mini and was walking towards the entrance when she saw a slightly built boy of about twelve straining to control an enormous black dog. The animal was too strong for him and broke loose. It bounded towards a little girl who was ahead of her parents and nearer to Claire. She immediately rushed forward to scoop the child into her arms, but, even so, the animal was quicker. It caught the small leg in its teeth before Claire could hold the child out of its reach.

The young parents screeched, the child screamed, and the dog was driven to a frenzy by the noise. It let go of the small girl's leg and made a lunge at Claire's face. It was so close that she could smell its breath, see its fierce eyes.

She lashed out with her free arm and knocked the dog on its nose. It fell back, but was lunging for another attack. Claire swung the child away so that her own back was to the dog and steeled herself for his bite, but it did not come. There was a loud thud followed by a shocked silence. Claire turned round.

The parents, a young couple in holiday clothes, stood with their mouths open in a silent scream. Mark was standing, his eyes as fierce as the dog's had been, looking down at the animal at his feet, a stout stick still held tightly in his hand. He was in shirt-sleeves, his tie discarded, his collar open, showing his strong neck.

'Whose dog is this?' His voice was full of anger.

Claire looked over the limp body of the child in her arms. 'There was a boy,' she whispered, her mouth dry with shock.

'No doubt he's skipped off,' said Mark gruffly.

Other holidaymakers were beginning to collect, drawn by the commotion. 'These dogs should be put down,' said one. 'You read something every day about them attacking a child,' said another.

'Thanks ever so, miss,' the young mother, who must have been in her early twenties, whispered, the eyes she looked at Claire with large with fright.

The young husband took the shocked child from Claire's arms. 'I don't know what we'd have done if you hadn't been so quick, miss,' he said, his face as shocked as his wife's.

'I don't either.' Mark's fierce voice sent the couple edging away from him. They looked as frightened of him as they had been of the dog.

Mark chose a sensible looking pensioner from the crowd.

'Would you phone for the police, please?' He reached into his trouser pocket and drew out some change which he gave to the grey-haired man.

'With pleasure,' the man said.

Blood was oozing from the child's leg and she was whimpering with shock. Turning to the parents, he said,

'I'm a doctor. Let me have a look at your little girl's leg.' His tone was gentle enough, but it was to Claire, still in uniform, that they looked.

She smiled. 'Yes, he really is,' she reassured them.

Still a little doubtfully, they allowed Mark to look at their daughter. There was a seat near by, and the couple sat down. Mark glanced at the crying child's leg, but he did not need to examine it, for its deformity told him all he needed to know.

'I'm afraid its broken,' he told the parents gently.

They stared at him in dismay. 'Oh!' they gasped in unison, their faces pale.

At that moment the police arrived and dispersed the crowd. Claire explained what had happened, and after their statements had been given the police sergeant said, 'Do you want an ambulance, Doctor?'

'No,' said Mark. 'I'll take them to hospital in my car.' He glanced at Claire. 'My staff nurse will accompany us.'

Claire knew why he had included her. The young couple had confidence in her, not him, so she nodded her agreement.

Mark brought his car across and helped the couple with the child into the back seat. Claire he put beside him.

In Casualty, she stayed with the child and her parents. 'It's the first time she's been in hospital.' Their faces were appalled.

'You mustn't worry,' she tried to reassure them. 'Young bones heal very quickly, and so will the bite.'

'But how will it affect her?' the young father asked anxiously. And when Claire frowned, not understanding, he said, 'Will she have nightmares?'

Claire was surprised at his intuitiveness, then shocked at how patronising she was. Just because he was young it did not mean he lacked understanding.

'She might,' Mark answered for her, when she was unable to reassure the father. How could she, when she was still hanted by a dream herself? 'But I hope not,' he smiled.

The positive way he spoke reassured them, and their faces cleared.

Mark glanced at Claire. 'You'll stay with Mr and Mrs Wood?' It was not an order, just an assumption.

'Yes,' said Claire.

'I'll drive you home afterwards. I've a few things to do here.'

'Thanks.'

She remained with the parents until the child had been seen by the doctor. When she saw that her support was no longer needed she left them and went to find Mark. He was still in Casualty, the sister told her, gesturing towards a cubicle.

Claire pushed aside the curtain. Mark was stitching a nasty cut on a child's foot.

'I wish people would put their litter in the bins provided,' he said, glancing up at Claire. 'Then this little fellow wouldn't have cut his foot on a piece of glass hidden in the sand.' He smiled at the seven-year-old, who was trying not to cry. 'This is the last one, Superman,' he said as he tied the knot and cut the thread, and smiled at the young staff nurse who was helping him. She blushed to almost the colour of her red hair, and Claire was jealous and appalled at her jealousy. She wasn't sure she could handle these new emotions entering her sterile life.

A grey-haired woman with a worried expression was holding the boy's hand. 'Thank you very much, Doctor,' she said gratefully. 'I don't know what his mother will say. I'm looking after Trevor while she's in hospital.' Her face brightened as she added, 'She's just had a little boy.'

'Congratulations, Trevor,' grinned Mark. 'A pal for you.'

'Better than a girl,' the boy grimaced. 'We've got one of those already.'

They all laughed, and their laughter swept away the child's fear. He grinned, not quite sure what the grown-ups were laughing at, but pleased he had amused them. It made him feel important.

Mark walked beside Claire to the car park. Claire glanced up at him, afraid she would see the hardness in his face that was there when she had told him where he had seen Steven, now that the emergency was over. Feeling her eyes on him, Mark looked down at her and smiled.

'That was a very brave thing to do,' he said as he

opened the passenger door for her. 'You could have been severely bitten.'

Claire's body relaxed as the tension drained out of it.

'I can't understand parents allowing a youngster to take out such a large dog.' They had left the car park by now and were in the High Street. 'A dog like that needs a man to handle it,' he said.

Claire glanced at Mark's arm. He would have no problem controlling such a dog, she thought. Then a vision of those arms holding her close flashed before her eyes and she had to run her tongue over her lips before she could say, 'Do you think they'll find the boy?' hoping her words would drown the thudding of her heart.

'Only if the dog had a name tag,' he said, swinging the car into his parking space.

As they left the car and crossed towards the entrance of their flats he said, 'Are you all right? You look a bit pale.' He took her elbow. 'Why, you're trembling.' His voice was full of concern. 'Probably delayed shock.'

The attack had shaken Claire, but it was Mark's nearness, the touch of his hand on her arm, that was the cause of her tremor.

'I'm fine,' she said, but the dryness of her mouth caused the words to come out as a whisper.

'What you need is a drink,' said Mark firmly, slipping his arm through hers and holding it close to his side.

The lift took them up to the third floor, one above hers. 'Look, I'll be fine.' She was beginning to panic.

'You don't need to worry.' His eyes were amused.

She wasn't afraid he would seduce her. She was afraid of the effect he was having on her, the melting she felt towards him, the desire that closed up her throat.

Then something suddenly occurred to her. Did he

have a wife? She looked up at his smiling face, and her whole body cried out for it not to be true.

'What is it?' Mark saw the distress in her eyes, and it puzzled him.

'I don't want to intrude,' Claire said the first thing that came into her mind.

He smiled. 'You won't. I live alone.'

Her lack of guile betrayed her into saying, 'Oh, you're not married, then?'

He grinned. 'No. I've been waiting for you.'

Claire blushed. He was teasing her, treating her like a child, and this made her mad and bitterness welled inside her because she wished it was true and he was not being facetious. The pain was so great that she said, her eyes cold, 'I don't appreciate jokes like that. Marriage is too serious an undertaking to be made fun of,' and she turned abruptly and left him on his landing.

But as she ran down the stairs, not bothering with the lift, she was miserable. What a stupid thing to say, patronising and childish, but it wasn't she who had spoken, it was her longing for him that had made her speak so.

The phone was ringing as she opened her door. She grabbed the receiver, her face full of joy, ready to apologise, do anything to see his smile, to hear his voice, to feel he did not dislike her.

'I'm —— ' she blurted into the mouthpiece.

'I'm what, pet?' Steven interrupted her.

'Oh, nothing,' she said, tears of frustration creeping into her eyes.

'You sound angry and upset.' Steven's voice was sharp. 'What's the matter?'

'Nothing.' Her reply was as sharp and brittle with it. The last person she could do with now was Steven.

'It's not like you to keep things from me.' He was disturbed.

'I'm not keeping anything from you,' she said, and felt guilty about the lie.

'There's no need to be cross with me.'

Claire heard the aggrieved tone in his voice, but she still did not tell him about Mark.

'I'm sorry,' she said, trying to keep the irritation out of her voice that his remark had occasioned. 'I'm just tired,' which was true.

'Been out a lot?' It was there again, the wounded note.

'No.' Her tone of voice implied that she did not like him questioning her about her movements.

He heard it, but ignored it. 'Don't lie to me, Claire.' It was he who was cross now. 'I phoned two or three times. . .' four, actually, but he didn't say so '. . .and there was no reply. That's why I phoned the ward, and I must say it was rotten of you not to come to the phone.'

He sounds just like a spoilt child, Claire thought.

'I can't just leave a post-operative patient to talk to you,' she said, aggravation strong in her voice. 'And by the way, we're not allowed to take calls on duty.' She hoped that would stop him making further calls to the ward, though she doubted it.

Steven apologised quickly, 'Sorry, pet.'

After a pause, Claire said, somewhat reluctantly, Steven thought, 'I was in London.'

'London? What were you doing there?' He was annoyed again. 'You should have told me.'

'Really, Steven, I don't have to tell you my every move.' He could hear the irritation in her voice.

'But I'm only concerned for your welfare.'

It sounded like a whine, but she controlled the impulse to scream at him abusively and said, 'I went up with a patient and stayed to special him.'

'Oh, I see.'

Claire wondered at the relief she heard in his voice. Surely he didn't think she was having an affair? And

Mark's face smiling down at her caught at her suddenly so that she could not speak for longing.

'Did you have a nice time in France?' She eventually managed to say, knowing too long a pause would make him suspicious.

'Yes. I'm in London now. How would you like a house guest for a few days?' Steven was bored, so he remembered that he was in love with Claire and thought it a good idea to resume his pursuit of her.

Claire did not want Steven in Whiteleigh now, so she said, 'I'll be working,' to put him off.

Her reply immediately fired his supposed love for her, and he wanted to know why she was so eager to put him off. 'That's all right,' he answered smoothly, not wanting her to see his suspicion. 'The sea air will do me good.' He knew that would sway her his way.

Claire had to laugh. It was a shared joke. She had a sudden memory of how, when they had been recovering from chicken-pox, his mother had said, 'I'm taking you both to Whiteleigh. The sea air will do you good.'

It had sounded so funny to the children that Steven and Claire had been convulsed with laughter. So now, every time they wanted to cheer themselves up, or make each other laugh, they used these words.

Now it broke the tension between them and Claire relented. 'I'm off this weekend,' she said.

'I'll come on Friday, then.'

Claire agreed. It was a relief to put down the receiver, though. She went and had a bath, and as she lay there she wondered what it would be like to be made love to, really made love to, and by Mark.

Intuitively she knew he would be a gentle yet passionate lover, and her skin grew hot as images of him touching her rose in the steam—misted, tantalising.

Quickly she pulled the plug and climbed out of the bath. Briskly she rubbed her skin with the towel as if by doing so it would dispel her wanton thoughts, but it only fired them. In bed, an unbearable longing, not for his touch, but for her to touch him, brought tears to her eyes. Was this love? Or was it just the awakening of her dormant sexuality, the melting of her frigidity?

Pushing these troubling thoughts aside, she turned the pillow and went to sleep. But even then his face appeared in her dreams — Mark's face, not that of her tormentor, and when she awoke she was a changed person and knew she would never have the nightmare again.

CHAPTER SIX

Two days later Claire had the two-to-ten shift. The weather had broken and clouds threatened rain. She hung up her mac and went into the office. There was no one there. Case-notes, charts, even the pens were in disarray.

Anxiety caught at her. What had happened? She went into the ward, but all seemed as usual. Those parents who were able to come in were playing with their children. One of them, a dark-haired mother of three whose youngest, a child of four, had had his tonsils removed yesterday, mouthed, 'Side-ward.'

Claire knew it was not Billy, as he had been moved to the main ward yesterday. It must be the burns case. She hurried to the side-ward and opened the door carefully. Mark's large figure seemed to fill the small room.

She had not seen him since the incident of the dog and the childish statement about facetiousness. Sister was with him. They were both gowned and so busy that they did not hear her come in.

The atmosphere in the room was tense, and Claire's heart contracted with apprehension and concern for the child as she suppressed her awareness of Mark and approached the bed. Quickly donning a gown and putting on a mask which was lying on the bedtable, she recalled how Louise had been burnt.

Louise's mother had left her alone for only a minute to answer the doorbell, but during that time the child, a three-year-old, had stood on her little chair and pulled a pan of boiling water over herself, scalding her

77

chest, abdomen, legs and one arm, but missing her face.

She had been rushed to Whiteleigh General and was to be transferred to a burns unit in London when her critical condition had improved. She had appeared to be progressing well and the drip had been discontinued. This was her second day.

'Oh, Claire.' Jessie's tense face relaxed. 'I'm glad you're here.'

Mark did not look up. He was busy trying to raise a vein in the small arm. Sighing, he said, 'No go,' as he released the tourniquet, throwing it down on the sheet. 'I'll have to do a cut-down.'

Quickly Claire washed her hands and spread out the packet on top of the trolley, being careful not to touch the sterile contents. Mark was washing his hands.

'We won't need a local,' he cast over his shoulder, 'She's unconscious.' His words were clipped, urgent. 'We'll lose her if we're not quick.'

Jessie was administering oxygen, holding the small mask over the flaccid face. Claire's anxiety for the little girl increased as she glanced towards the child. Louise looked lifeless.

Claire opened a packet of sterile gloves and tipped them on to the trolley. She had chosen the large size and they just fitted, but the size of the surgeon's hands did not affect the delicacy of his work. His fingers moved with quick assurance, and Claire was cutting the last stitch holding the small wound together and the needle in place within seconds. Her admiration for his skill showed in her eyes, but he was too intent on ensuring his work was perfect to see it.

Placing a small dressing over the wound, he said, 'Help me to bandage it, please.' His voice was harsh with anxiety. Claire doubted if he knew she was there, and this was confirmed by the surprise in his eyes when he looked up and saw her holding out the splint.

A fleeting pleasure at the sight of her was quickly squashed as he applied himself once more to bandaging the splint into place with Claire supporting the arm.

Claire relaxed. He must have forgotten her outburst.

'How is she, Sister?' Mark asked in an even tone, but his face was tense.

Jessie was trying to find a pulse, and her face was as tense as Mark's. 'I can't find one,' she said, glancing up at him, her eyes fearful.

He looked up at the bag of fluid. 'We may need to give her plasma again.' There was a worried frown between his brows as he bent to examine the child. Her skin was clammy and pale. She was flaccid and lifeless.

Narrowing his eyes, Mark peered more closely, and detected a change. Only his years of experience made him aware of it, for it was not something obvious, more a certainty. Claire felt it too.

Then Jessie said, barely able to control her excitement, 'I can feel a pulse.' There were tears in her eyes as she looked at Mark and Claire. 'It's weak and thready, but it's there.' Her face was radiant, and Claire knew how she felt, for she was feeling the same.

Mark grinned at them both. Then his face straightened.

'We're not out of the woods yet.'

'But there's hope now.' Claire smiled at him, but he was bending to the child again.

'With good nursing, yes.' He looked up. 'At least her face wasn't burnt. Louise won't have people looking at her in horror.'

Claire's mouth gaped with shock. Then she realised the reference was not made especially for her, but just a general observation. He wasn't even looking at her, his eyes were on Jessie.

'That's a blessing,' said Jessie, her fingers still feeling the pulse. 'It's improving.' Her smile was broad, and Mark and Claire smiled back.

The doctor and the two nurses concentrated on the child, willing her to improve. Her skin had lost its lifeless look; it was still pale, but this time it was not the paleness of death.

Louise opened her eyes and whimpered. Jessie grabbed the bowl from the locker, and, whipping the mask from the child's face, just caught the vomit in the bowl before it was inhaled. Claire pushed past Mark to hold Louise's head. Jessie murmured soothing words as she bathed the little girl's now flushed face.

'We may have to change her antibiotics,' said Mark thoughtfully. 'And we'll sedate her.'

Jessie and Claire, together, turned the child's damp pillow.

'I want you to stay with her until we can get a nurse to special her,' said Jessie, glancing at Claire.

'Mummy, Mummy,' Louise whimpered.

'Shall I fetch her?' asked Claire, compassion naked in her eyes.

Jessie nodded.

'I'll look in later,' said Mark to the ward sister. Then, turning to Claire, he said, 'Don't hesitate to call for me.'

She nodded, and could not stop herself from watching as he removed his mask and gown and threw them into the bin provided. Would they still hold the scent of him? wondered Claire. Would they? Her body leaned forward, and it was the closing of the door that brought her back to where she was.

'What a good job Mr Stanger was in the ward when Louise collapsed. She might have died while we waited for the doctor.' Jessie sighed. There was only so much a nurse was qualified to do.

Claire went to fetch the mother. The young woman's hair looked as lifeless as her daughter's, and the lines on Mrs Morgan's face had deepened. She seemed older than her twenty-five years.

Claire put on her best encouraging smile. 'Louise has improved,' she said.

Tears filled Janet Morgan's eyes. 'Thank God!' she whispered. 'I don't think I could have lived with myself if she had died.'

Her face was so stricken that Claire rushed to put an arm round her shoulders. 'You mustn't blame yourself.' Claire put all her energies into reassuring the mother. 'The handle of the pan was turned away. You weren't to know Louise would pull her chair over to look in the pot.'

Janet closed her eyes. 'But I should have.' Her voice was full of agony. She threw back her head. 'Oh!' she wailed. 'I can't bear it.'

Claire gripped her shoulders and made the mother look at her. 'Going to pieces isn't going to help Louise,' she said in a firm voice. 'She's going to need strength and calmness from you.'

Janet gave a ragged sigh and raised her distressed face to Claire's serious one. 'I'll try, Staff.'

Claire smiled and patted her shoulder and took her to Louise's bedside.

The little girl's condition improved throughout the day. Mark returned later, and Claire handed him the charts. Flipping through them, he said, 'Good,' and handed them back to her. 'She's coming along nicely, Mrs Morgan.' He smiled encouragingly at Janet.

The three of them were standing at the foot of the bed with Mark facing the women. He was wearing a navy blue tie which made his eyes appear bluer. He was so handsome that even Janet blushed, and, for herself, Claire's heart seemed to swell with — love? Or just admiration?

Mark smiled at Claire. How incredible that just that smile could lighten her day.

'Louise should make a good recovery, Mrs Morgan,'

said Mark. 'Is your husband coming in today?' He smiled kindly.

'Yes.' Janet managed to smile back. 'I phoned him as soon as Sister told me about Louise's relapse, but he was too far away to come immediately. He's a lorry driver,' she explained. 'But he should be here any minute now.'

'Good.'

Claire went with Mark to the door. 'Let me know if you need me,' he said softly and with such meaning in his eyes that she knew he was not only referring to the patient, and she blushed. 'I'll let Sister know where I'll be.'

She thanked him and expected him to leave, and had her hand on the doorknob ready to close it after him, but he still lingered. She looked at him enquiringly.

'I'm sorry if I sounded facetious the other day,' he said, his eyes serious. 'You were quite right—marriage is a serious business and not to be undertaken lightly.' He smiled gently and touched her face. She could feel an underlying intenseness in the way he leaned towards her. 'But I wasn't being facetious, Claire.' His voice was soft and seductive, his eyes serious, and her heart thudded.

She was excited yet depressed. How could she cope, inexperienced as she was, with this vital, sexually magnetic man? And was he sincere? What about the blonde young woman? So she smiled coolly and said lightly,

'We all dream of marrying handsome doctors, we nurses, so you'd better watch out. I might take you up on your offer.' And she grinned, hoping he would take her words as a joke.

This was not the place to continue such a conversation so Mark just smiled. A whimper from the bed drew Claire's eyes.

'I'll be in later,' said Mark and left.

Louise's father was there when Mark returned. He was a big man with a heavy face and bushy eyebrows which gave him a louring appearance, but it was deceptive. He was a loving husband and an adoring father.

'We'll be moving Louise to the burns unit at. . .' here Mark named the London hospital. '. . .as soon as your daughter's condition is stable.' He smiled reassuringly.

'What caused Louise's relapse?' David Morgan asked.

'Sometimes toxaemia may occur two days following a severe burn,' Mark explained. Then seeing the frown on the man's face he said, 'That means there are poisons in the blood.'

David Morgan nodded.

A short time later Mark left.

The rest of Claire's shift was hectic. Jessie stayed on duty so that Claire could special Louise until another agency nurse, Mrs Clark, was brought in at six o'clock. This lady was used regularly by the hospital and knew the small patients; she had been on duty yesterday and was familiar with Louise. Margaret Clark could only work in the evening when her husband was at home to look after their children.

Claire came off duty at ten-thirty. She had spent the time since Jessie had gone off in catching up on the paperwork for Jessie as well as supervising the ward.

She had made time to instruct Jean Johnson in how to care for Billy when he was discharged. 'You may still need to use elbow restraints at night,' she warned the mother. 'And you'll have to prevent him from putting his fingers into his mouth, as you already know.' Claire smiled. 'It'll be difficult to stop him from sucking and blowing, but his stitch line has to be protected.' She stroked Billy's hair from off his forehead. 'I don't need to tell you to continue with the soft food diet.'

'No, but thanks anyway.' Jean gave Claire a grateful smile. 'And I'll be sure to keep his mouth clean after every meal.'

'Good.' Claire studied Jean's face, noting the anxiety the mother was trying to hide. 'You might like to contact an association called CLAPA, for short. It's the Cleft Lip and Palate Association, and it's a support group for parents with children like Billy. It's based in Newcastle, but does have local groups. I'll give you the number of the London one.'

Jean's face cleared. 'Oh, thanks. That'll be a great help.'

So it was a very tired Claire who approached her car. The dull sky made it quite dark. A large figure in a man's jacket came forward, and Claire thought it was Mr Morgan until Mark said, 'I was hoping for a lift.'

'Been waiting long?' she asked drily.

'Half an hour.'

Claire could just see, in the half-light, the grin on his face.

She laughed happily. 'Do you think you'll fit?' she asked as she unlocked the Mini, then laughed again as he telescoped himself into the passenger-seat.

'I'll have you know that I used to rocket around in one of these when I was a student.' His voice held that 'so there!' note.

Claire had a mental picture of a younger Mark with a more mobile face, with fewer stress lines beside the eyes in the driving seat, and she wished she had known him then. She smiled to herself, for she would only have been about eleven. Mark must be about thirty-five.

'Is it a shareable joke?' Mark's voice broke into her reverie.

'It's not a joke really.' And then because she did not

want him to think that she was laughing at him, she
said,

'I was just imagining what you must have looked like
then.'

'It *was* amusing.' He laughed. 'I was all gangling
limbs.'

She gave him a disbelieving glance.

'It's true — take it from me.'

A vision of Mark, vulnerable and young, rose before
her on the windscreen. The car swerved slightly.

'Like me to drive?' Mark asked, too casually.

'No, thank you,' she said firmly, and concentrated
on the road.

The rain which had threatened all day had started
and she had the headlights on before they reached the
flats. Mark whipped off his jacket and held it over their
heads as they ran from the car. It was a laughing pair
who reached the protection of the hall.

Claire expected Mark to remove his jacket from
above them, but he still held it there umbrellaing them.
The rain had soaked the grey tweed material, and a
damp earthy smell rose from its fibres. It excited Claire.
There was something primitive about the scent and the
sheltering arms. Mark's nearness and the touch of his
body close to hers stirred her blood. She looked up
into his face and saw in the soft light naked desire in
his eyes, and her excitement increased.

'Claire,' he whispered, and dropped the jacket so
that it settled over them like a tent. He took her into
his arms and kissed her.

She responded eagerly. Never had a kiss aroused her
as this one did. Her whole body flamed into life, her
skin burned with desire — a desire for more than just a
kiss. Her arms went round his neck, her grip tightened.
She was lost — lost. When he released her she still kept
her hands on his shoulders, loath to lose touch.

His voice was thick as he said, 'I can forgive you

anything when you kiss me like that. Even your distaste for disfigurement. . .' It had lingered at the back of his mind like an irritation and came out of his mouth without him thinking.

Claire threw off his jacket, her eyes blazing.

'That's very generous of you.' Her voice was clipped. 'Did you ever think that there might be another reason for my expression that day?'

Mark frowned. 'What other reason could there be?' Then his mouth gaped. 'You mean I was the reason?' And when she did not answer because she did not know how to, he said, 'Why?'

Hearing the vulnerability beneath that one word and feeling how it tore at her heart, Claire resolved to tell Mark about the dream.

'You. . .'

'So it was me,' Mark interrupted. Anger lay behind the bewilderment in his eyes. 'Well. . .' His tone was disdainful. 'You seem to have overcome your aversion to me, or were you just putting on an act just now?'

'How can you —— ?' Claire was going to add, 'think that,' when a draught of air was followed by,

'There you are, Claire. I came earlier, but you were out.' And Steven approached them.

Mark and Claire were so engrossed in each other that it took a moment for them to comprehend what he was saying. Then Claire, in her distress, ran over to him and took his arm. 'Steven!' she exclaimed with more delight than usual.

'Aren't you going to introduce us?' asked Steven, looking at Mark, his face expressionless, his tone cool.

'Oh — er — yes,' Claire stuttered, and glanced at Mark's grim face. 'Mark, this is my cousin Steven West.' Her face was very pale. 'Steven — Mark Stanger, my ward consultant.'

Steven nodded, but did not hold out his hand, and nor did Mark. Dislike crackled between the two men.

'And were you consulting now?' Steven asked his cousin, his voice sarcastic. 'It looked like an argument to me.'

Claire was so upset that she did not hear the mockery in Steven's tone. 'It was just a difference of opinion,' she said, smiling into her cousin's eyes.

Steven's face softened. 'Shall we go up, pet?' he said, ignoring Mark.

Mark picked up his jacket and followed them to the lift. Steven raised an eyebrow, his expression haughty.

'I don't recall asking you to join us,' he said.

'I live here.' Mark's tone was abrupt.

'Oh, yes?' Steven was not pleased.

Claire was disconcerted when Mark entered the lift with them. She had thought he would have preferred the stairs, and she would have been happier if he had, for the touch of his lips still lingered and she knew she would never be able to smell that earthy scent again without his face appearing before her and feel the touch of his lips on hers.

It seemed as if he deliberately placed himself on her other side. Her arm was in Steven's, but her awareness was for Mark. His face was sharp in her memory, as sharp as that other face — the one in her dream.

The lift stopped at her floor, and Claire felt as if she had left part of herself behind when she stepped from it.

'Give me your key,' said Steven, and Claire could hear the tension in his voice as she handed it to him.

Once in the flat, to delay Steven's questions which she knew would come, Claire asked, 'Have you eaten?' as she switched on the lights.

'Yes, earlier.' Steven's voice was still tight.

'Well, I haven't, except for a cup of tea.' She wished he wasn't there so that she could be miserable on her own. 'I'm going to make a cheese omelette. Would you like one?'

It was a speciality of hers, and Steven said, 'Yes,' eagerly and grinned. He looked so like the boy she used to play with that she laughed. Perhaps he would take her mind off Mark's words. Perhaps he would lift her misery a bit.

By the time Claire had made the omelettes and set them on the coffee table, it was eleven-thirty. Steven had lit the fire and the room was warm and cosy. The table lamps and drawn curtains added an intimacy to the atmosphere which Claire was not too sure about.

They were sitting on the couch drinking their coffee after their meal when Steven said, 'So tell me about this Mark Stanger.'

'I did tell you.' Claire tried to speak calmly. 'He's the consultant on my ward.'

'Wasn't he with that scarred girl at the Haven? The man in your dream?' He was being sarcastic now, but Claire did not hear this; she only heard his reference to Mark's companion, and this brought the discord between Mark and herself into the room like an univited guest.

'Yes,' she said shortly, not wanting to encourage this line of conversation.

She was collecting the coffee-cups on to the tray, and Steven took it from her.

'A bit weird, being attracted to this man, then,' Steven remarked, following her into the kitchen.

She swung round. 'Who said I was attracted to Mark?' Her tone was over-emphatic and convinced Steven that his cousin was more involved with this doctor than he had realised. He was furious, but hid it behind a smile.

'No need to fly off the handle at me' he said.

Claire was washing the dishes. 'How long are you staying?' she asked in a sharp voice.

'Want me to go already?'

She had her back to him and did not see the anger in

his face, the desire in his eyes. It was concealed as she swung round, soapsuds flying from her hands.

'Don't be silly, Steven,' she snapped. 'Whatever's the matter with you?'

'It isn't what's the matter with me.' Steven's anger was showing now as he brushed the gossamer bubbles from his jacket. 'You're the one who's changed.' His face was red. 'It's that man,' he accused her, working himself into a fury. Visions of Claire lying in Mark's arms, the woman Steven thought he loved being caressed by another man, made his face ugly. 'Has he taken you into his bed yet?'

Claire's wet hand left an imprint of her fingers on her cousin's cheek as she slapped him. Then both her hands flew to her mouth in horror. This was Steven — her childhood friend, her Steven.

'So it's true.' Steven was incensed. He reached for her and pulled her into his arms, desire flaring in his eyes.

Claire was alarmed. 'You're hurting me,' she protested sharply, trying to push him away, not believing what she saw in his face.

His grip tightened and his lips came down on hers in a kiss that was an assault, not only on her as a woman, but on her trust in him.

She sagged with shock, and this unbalanced Steven so that he released her. She fled out of the flat and up the stairs, not daring to wait for the lift, knowing that Steven, blind to everything but his desire, would catch her there and pull her back into the flat.

What a good job she knew where Mark lived. She did not think their recent quarrel would cause him to reject her. She only knew that he would protect her.

She rang the bell and knocked on the door, glancing towards the stairs in case Steven had pursued her, her anxiety etched on her face.

CHAPTER SEVEN

MARK opened the door. Claire gazed at him blank-faced. What explanation could she give for her precipitate call? She could not tell him about Steven.

Mark's eyes narrowed. He noted her distress, her dishevelment, her hesitation, and knew he was not the cause. It must be her cousin Steven who had wrought this change in her. Mark was still smarting from the realisation that it was he who had caused Claire's look of horror that day at the Haven, but, on reflection, he had decided that, whatever it was about him that had made her fear him, it was no longer there.

'I. . .' There was a pause, then she said in a rush, 'Could you let me have a cup of sugar?' Her voice was as strained as her face.

'Come in,' he said, opening the door wider and not mentioning her lack of a cup. 'I'll fetch it.'

Claire stepped into the flat, and was immediately comforted. His jacket hung on a hook, his doctor's bag was on the hall table. Steven could not take her from here. Her ears strained for the sound of his footsteps outside the door.

Mark was back too soon with the cup of sugar.

'Here you are —' he wanted to add, 'my darling', but did not think it would help her just now if he declared his love and longing.

'Thanks.' She avoided his eyes. She did not want him to see her reluctance to leave. 'I'll return the cup.'

'Any time,' he said, showing her out.

Claire gave an absent smile and hurried away, so she did not see the narrowing of his eyes and the concern in their depths.

It was with some trepidation that she approached her front door. It was closed, and she did not have her key. Feeling rather stupid, she rang the bell. It was not answered. She pushed the door and it swung open. The light was still on in the hall.

Summoning her courage, she called, 'Steven!'

There was no reply, and, sighing with relief, Claire went into the lounge. A piece of paper was lying on the coffee table. She picked it up and read,

> Claire, I hope you can forgive me. I don't know what came over me. I think it was seeing you with that man that made me realise how much I love you, and I was insanely jealous. I've gone to London and will stay at my club. I'll phone you from there.
> Love,
> Steven.

'Everything all right?'

Claire swung round, her face white with fright. Mark was standing in the lounge doorway.

'You could give someone a heart attack doing that', she snapped, her eyes wide.

'Well, at least I didn't make you faint this time.' He grinned. 'You really should close your front door.' His face was serious now, as he glanced about the lounge. 'Your cousin?'

'Had to go up to London,' she said evenly, screwing Steven's note into a ball.

'Really?' Mark raised an eyebrow. 'Sudden, wasn't it?'

'So what?' She was cross and upset at the same time.

He did not press her. 'So do you still want the sugar?' His eyes were amused.

Claire was still holding the cup. She looked up into his smiling face. 'Er. . .' She looked blank, too tired to think, then she said, 'Not now.' Should she ask him to stay for coffee?

'I won't stay for coffee.' He had read her expressive face. 'You look as if you need some sleep.'

He looked at her so gently that she could have cried and wanted to throw herself into his arms, but there was a tenseness between them that she felt unable to break.

At the front door, Mark said, 'I'll always be here if you need me, Claire.'

The softening of his face, the gentleness of his voice, swept away the tension. It was as if there had never been any dissent between them — no hurtful words spoken only that evening.

'I'll remember that when I need a cup of sugar,' she said, leaning towards him her lips moist with longing.

A door opening on her landing and a voice saying, 'Some people are trying to sleep,' prevented him from kissing her.

'Goodnight, Claire.' He made her name sound like a caress.

It was Claire's weekend off, and she spent it thinking of how she would deal with Steven. It must be firmly. She had recovered from the shock and regretted not having faced him at the time. Now she had to find a way to show him that he was not in love with her, but she dreaded his phone call. Mark had also been in her thoughts far too much.

She spent the morning doing her washing and going to the supermarket to replenish her stock of food. After a light lunch, she was about to watch the afternoon film when the phone rang. It was two-thirty.

She let it ring for a while. Then, deciding she would have to speak to Steven some time, she lifted the receiver, tensing herself as she did so.

'Miss Forrest?' It was the senior nursing officer's distinctive voice.

'Yes,' said Claire, relieved that it was not Steven.

'I'm afraid there's been an accident. . .' Claire's mouth went dry. Had Steven crashed his car? Had his emotional state —— ? 'We're calling in all the available staff.' She breathed again. 'A bus bringing children to Whiteleigh for their Sunday-school picnic crashed at the terrible junction leading into Montgomery Road. We don't have the details yet, but it's serious. Mr Stanger has gone out with the flying squad. I know you're an agency nurse but could you come to Casualty as soon as possible?'

'I'll come at once,' promised Claire.

She had changed and was in her car within minutes. The traffic was heavy, so it took her longer than she would have wished to reach the hospital, and when she did the parking spaces were full, so that she had to leave her car at the roadside, which delayed her further.

An ambulance, it's siren dying from a wail to a whisper, drew up at the accident and emergency entrance at the same time that she did. The ambulance-men were flinging back the doors in a moment. Mark leapt out, streaks of blood on his white coat making a crazy pattern on it.

He helped the ambulancemen convert the stretcher into a trolley and they rushed forward with the patient. Mark did not seem surprised to see Claire at his elbow, and handed her the intravenous plasma to hold. He wanted to keep the oxygen mask more firmly over the child's face.

'We'll take him straight to Theatre.' His voice was urgent. Halting the trolley, he lifted the mask and checked the child's colour. Claire could see the airway keeping the passages open. 'As far as I can determine. . .' Mark's words were disjointed as they hurried forward once more '. . .he's bleeding internally. Most likely from a ruptured spleen.'

The casualty department was crowded with crying

children in torn T-shirts, screaming children with minor cuts caused by the shattering glass patterning their faces. Those parents who had been contacted or who had accompanied their children were comforting their little ones and giving what reassurance they could to those whose parents had still to come.

'Your mummy will be here soon,' a young redheaded mother with a shocked face was saying, her arm around a crying child with its arm in a sling.

'But when?' The little girl who was five that day, wailed, her good arm hugging a small red bag.

'Soon, Nicky,' a cheerful nurse said. 'What a lovely bag you have! Can I see it?' She hoped to distract the distressed child.

'No!' Nicky said petulantly, holding the bag away from the outstretched hand.

The nurse smiled and went to attend to another child. Nurses and doctors tried in calm voices to soothe the frightened youngsters. The WRVS ladies had arrived to open the canteen, their numbers increased to help with comforting the parents, releasing the nurses to attend to the injured.

'Ah, Staff Nurse Forrest.' The SNO came out of the lift Mark and Claire were waiting for. She helped push the trolley in and stayed with them as it ascended.

'You'll have to assist Mr Stanger in Theatre,' she said as the doors opened on the next floor.

Mark glanced at the SNO in astonishment. 'Surely the theatre sisters have arrived?'

'This is a small hospital, Mr Stanger.' Mrs Godfrey was not intimidated by Mark's tone. They were pushing the trolley towards the theatre. 'One of my theatre sisters is away this weekend, and we're trying to contact her. The other two sisters are operating now.'

'But Staff here isn't qualified,' Mark protested as they reached the theatre.

'Miss Forrest has six months' theatre experience,'

the SNO informed him. 'We're all stretched to the limit.'

Claire was horrified. She had thought, following her RGN training, that she would like to specialise in theatre work and had been accepted at her training hospital, but had soon realised that her life was even more sterile. She missed the personal contact with the patients and the warmth of giving. It was eighteen months since she had last been in Theatre.

'I'm sure you'll manage very well, won't you, Staff?' Mrs Godfrey gave Claire a look that expected a positive reply.

'I'll do my best,' said Claire, hoping her nervousness did not show.

The SNO left with a smile on her face which was not reflected on Mark's. It did not help Claire's confidence to know that he had doubts about her ability, and her confidence suffered another blow when she found James Robinson was the anaesthetist.

'Good job you told me you were visiting your sister this weekend, James.' Mark grinned at him.

'Me and my big mouth,' grimaced James, but he smiled.

Claire knew he was an excellent anaesthetist who did not mind being called out. She had heard that his wife was a nagger, and perhaps that was why he was always making advances to attractive nurses whom she met during his work. His eyes were running over Claire now, bringing a blush to her cheek.

'I hear you're to scrub,' he said. 'Wait until you see her in that thin gown.' He could not disguise the lust in his eyes as they rested on her, even though he was speaking to Mark.

'I suggest you keep your mind on your work.' Mark's voice was grim with disapproval.

Claire cast him a grateful glance, but James ignored Mark's tone and said,

'Of course, you came after Claire had left Theatres.' He was busy attending to a patient as he spoke.

'Oh, shut up!' snapped Claire, her voice full of disgust.

'And I endorse that,' said Mark, grinning at her before going to scrub.

A gowned nurse passed him. 'I've prepared the theatre,' she said. 'The packs just need opening.'

Claire was relieved that another woman had appeared. It would prevent further innuendoes from James, so she smiled.

'Thank goodness,' she said, but her smile became fixed when she saw the resentment on the other nurse's face. 'I hope you'll guide me,' she said diplomatically.

'You'd better scrub.' There was no relenting in the nurse's tone, or a lessening of hostility on her face. 'I don't know why you're assisting Mr Stanger. I could have, just as well.'

'This is hardly the time to discuss your capabilities, Nurse,' Claire said coldly. 'A small boy's life should be our main concern.' And she went to scrub, not waiting to see what effect her words had had.

Mark was leaving the scrub-room as Claire entered.

'You'd better be quick,' he said in a sharp voice, 'or I'll start without you.' And he was gone.

Claire was not going to let him fluster her, she was flustered enough already. She tucked her hair under her theatre cap and scrubbed meticulously. Moments later she was gowned and ready to assist him.

Quickly she checked the instruments.

'Ready?' Mark's voice was impatient.

'Yes, sir,' she answered smartly.

An amused twinkle lit his eyes, but he did not speak, just looked at the anaesthetist, who nodded.

His hand shot out, and Claire slapped the scalpel handle on to it.

It was amazing how it came back. She supposed it must be like riding a bicycle — you never forgot. Her anticipation of Mark's every move raised his eyebrows in appreciation.

Ten minutes later he said, 'You'll have to assist here.' His brow wrinkled in frustration. 'Where the hell is Ronnie?'

They were almost finished when Ronnie North appeared.

'Need any help?' he asked laconically from the door.

'We've been managing quite well without it, but now you're here — scrub.' Mark's tone was dry.

Within minutes, a masked and gowned Ronnie joined them. 'You haven't introduced me to the new theatre sister,' he said, taking over from Claire.

'Miss Forrest,' Mark said shortly.

Ronnie's mask hid his gaping mouth. 'Oh!' was all he could think of to say.

Gowned beneath the hot lights, the theatre staff looked like creatures from another planet; one where green creatures lived who had only eyes.

A little while later, Mark's voice barked,

'Spencer-Wells, quickly! There's a bleeding point here.'

Claire slapped the forceps into his outstretched hand. His gloves were bloodied and slippery, but he grasped it. He stopped the bleeding, and the flare of tension that had gripped them subsided.

'Mop Mr Stanger's brow, please, Nurse.' Claire nodded in his direction and received a grateful glance from Mark.

Later he said, 'We're almost ready to close,' and sounded more relaxed. 'Swab count, please.'

The bloodstained swabs tallied with the number used, so Mark closed the wound. 'Cut.' Ronnie snipped the string of the last suture.

Mark looked at James. 'How is he?'

'OK. His blood-pressure's a little low, but the blood transfusion will fix that.'

They all helped transfer the boy to the trolley.

'Go with him.' Mark nodded at Ronnie.

Claire and Mark left James checking his anaesthetic machine and went into the scrub-room. Mark stripped off his gown and threw it with his mask and cap into the bin. His chest was damp with perspiration, and Claire's heartbeat quickened. She wasn't aware that she had moved closer to him drawn by her yearning, until he said,

'The bin's over there,' nodded towards where his green gown hung half in and half out of the laundry backet.

Oh, how I'd like him to kiss me, Claire thought, the wish so intense she was unable to speak for a moment. Then, taking a deep breath, she said,

'I've only got my bra and pants on,' and blushed.

'I'm not shy,' said Mark, grinning.

'Well, I am,' Claire said firmly, but smiled as well.

'What a shame,' he teased, and turning his back he said, 'I'm going for a shower,' adding with a quick glance over his shoulder and a challenge in his eyes, 'Coming?'

Claire's longing was so great that she almost accepted, but she couldn't, she just couldn't. It wasn't because she was a prude. It was because she could not bear to feel the water pouring over her, so she said,

'No, thanks,' and thought she saw mockery in his eyes before he left her, but how could she explain?

Her fear of water was linked with the dream and that face. Quickly she suppressed the hazy pictures threatening to rise from the past. They had been crowding her since she had met Mark, clamouring to be recognised.

Claire shivered, even though she was hot and sticky. She went to change, and was about to leave the theatre when the phone rang.

'I'll get it,' she called.

It was the SNO.

'I'd be grateful if you'd continue in Theatre for now, Miss Forrest. I haven't been able to get hold of Miss Barton yet.'

'Very well, Mrs Godfrey,' said Claire, knowing she couldn't refuse.

She assisted Mark with four more operations, and the rapport between them grew with each successive case. There was only time for a quick coffee at six.

They were both tired and hungry when the last case, a badly lacerated boy who required the careful removal of glass splinters from his arms and legs, went down to the ward.

The SNO came into the theatre as Claire was sorting out the instruments. The older woman's face looked as fresh as when Claire had seen it hours ago.

'Mr Stanger's full of praise for the way you've coped,' Mrs Godfrey told her. 'And so am I. It would have created many difficulties if you hadn't made yourself available. Thank you very much,' she added sincerely.

Claire blushed. The SNO's words were welcome, but it was Mark's praise that thrilled her. It showed he appreciated her as a nurse.

'Is the emergency over now?' asked Claire.

'Yes. Those not badly hurt have gone home, and those who had to be admitted have been accommodated here.' Sadness touched Mrs Godfrey's eyes. 'The bus driver's on the critical list with a fractured skull. He's still unconscious.' Then her face brightened. 'At least the accident wasn't his fault, so when he does come round he won't be haunted.'

Claire was glad. She was only too well aware of what memories could do.

Mrs Godfrey paused at the theatre door. 'Well, at least you have a day off tomorrow to recover,' she said, leaving with a smile.

The casualty entrance was the nearest to where Claire had parked her car. She was making her way there when Mark swung into step beside her.

'On your way home?' he queried.

She nodded.

'I know this Italian restaurant. . .'

'Luigi's?' Claire interrupted him, smiling.

'You know it too.' The tired lines about his eyes crinkled into a smile. 'How would you like me to treat you?'

'I'd like it very much.' Then she grimaced. 'But I'm not really dressed for the occasion.'

'I'm sure Luigi won't mind,' he grinned.

Suddenly the differences between Mark and her cousin impressed itself upon her. Steven would have been horrified if she even suggested accompanying him to a restaurant in uniform, and thinking of that reminded her that he was still to phone.

'Is your car here?' asked Mark. They were out of the hospital now. When she replied in the affirmative, he said, 'We'll take mine and come back for yours later.'

Claire was so hungry that she willingly agreed.

Sitting beside him in the passenger-seat, she ran her fingers through her hair. 'I came without my bag,' she said. 'I hope I don't look too scruffy.'

'You'll never look that,' said Mark, and the admiration in his eyes made her blush. It was so relaxing to be with someone who did not always demand that she look glamorous as Steven did.

They came to the junction where the accident had happened. The police were directing the traffic into a single lane. The bus still lay on its side, its windows shattered, but the lorry which had caused the accident was not there.

'It must have been towed away,' said Mark, his thoughts similar to Claire's.

She shivered as a vision of what had occurred caught at her imagination.

'The sooner we get some food into you the better.' Mark had misunderstood the reason for her tremor. 'Your blood sugar's low.'

'It certainly is, Doctor,' she quipped. 'And I expect yours is as well.'

She could see his grin, as the daylight was still good, even though it was ten o'clock. They were soon at Luigi's and Mark was lucky enough to find a parking space.

As they stepped through the doors into the cheerful atmosphere of check tablecloths and Chianti bottles with candles in them, an olive-skinned man, round of figure with receding hair, came forward, a smile lighting his dark eyes.

'How nice to see you again, Miss Claire,' he greeted her.

'Thank you, Luigi. It's nice to be here,' she said with a smile.

'And you too, Doctor.'

'Thanks, Luigi,' Mark smiled. 'Do you have a free booth for us?'

Luigi was looking at Claire as he said, 'For Miss Claire, anything is possible.'

'Oh!' Mark's eyes were amused, and Claire laughed.

They sat opposite each other on red vinyl seating.

'Mr Steven well?' asked Luigi as he handed them a menu each.

Claire had not realised how happy she was until Luigi mentioned Steven. She had never felt this way with him. The mention of her cousin tightened her face.

'He's fine,' she answered.

'I think a bottle of Chianti would go down well with spaghetti bolognese,' said Mark, seeing her disquiet.

'I'm sure it will suit your choice as well.' He smiled encouragingly at her.

Claire relaxed. She wasn't going to let thoughts of her cousin spoil her evening. 'I'll have the spaghetti as well,' she said, smiling up at Luigi.

'I like this place,' she told Mark as Luigi departed.

'You come here with your cousin?' Mark asked.

'Yes,' she said, not realising how her eyes had clouded.

Luigi brought the wine, and, after he had left, Mark raised his glass to Claire, his eyes soft in the candlelight. 'Here's looking at you, kid,' he said, imitating Humphrey Bogart's voice.

Claire laughed, but beneath her laughter she was remembering the last time she had been to Luigi's with Steven and how sharp her cousin had been with the waiter.

'I want Luigi to serve us,' he had said arrogantly. And when the waiter had told Steven that Luigi was with another customer, Steven had said, 'Oh, very well,' in a petulant manner.

Claire had been furious, and had said so after they had left the restaurant. Steven had not spoken to her for a week after that. He hated to be criticised.

Their meal arrived soon afterwards. Claire was twisting her spaghetti round her fork when Mark said,

'You've had a row with your cousin, haven't you?'

She paused with her fork halfway to her mouth.

'You could say that,' she agreed, popping the spaghetti into her mouth, to prevent her having to elucidate.

Mark was looking at her thoughtfully. He had not touched his food. 'When you came to the flat last night. . .'

He was looking at her so sympathetically and she felt so alone with her problem with no one to confide in, and her resistance was lowered because she was tired, so she brushed her loyalty to Steven aside and told Mark what had happened. 'He was jealous,' she said by way of an excuse.

Mark showed no surprise. It was as if he had suspected.

'What are you going to do?' he asked gently.

Claire sighed. 'Wait for his phone call, I suppose.'

'Well, if there's anything I can do. . .' he smiled.

She grinned back. 'You have already,' she told him, and, seeing his puzzled frown, continued, 'You've fed me.'

'I could do a lot more for you,' he said cheekily.

Did she imagine the wistfulness behind his smile? Was he courting her? If only it was true. Was it true?

She regarded him with serious blue eyes.

Luigi came up at that moment to enquire if they would like a sweet. After they had chosen, he said,

'How is Miss Susie, Dr Mark?'

Mark's mind was on Claire and he answered absent-mindedly, 'She's fine. She couldn't come tonight.'

'Perhaps next time,' said Luigi, not realising how his words had swept Claire's happiness away. It faded like the passing of summer, and the coldness of winter settled on her awakening love for Mark. He had only asked her to come because this Susie was unavailable. What an innocent she was to suppose Mark was free. Susie was an attractive girl in spite of her deformity, which Claire knew could be corrected with plastic surgery.

Mark felt Claire's withdrawal, but did not understand the reason for it. Susie meant nothing to him emotionally, so he did not equate his mention of her with Claire's change towards him.

The strawberries and cream which arrived later tasted like dust. Their conversation was stilted, and Claire refused his offer of coffee, only wanting to leave and return home to lick her wounds.

She was quiet in the car. The harbour lights seemed to be winking at her in mockery as they came into view.

'Tired?' Mark tried to break the barrier between them.

'Just a bit.'

'Susie and I are going sailing tomorrow,' he said as he headed back towards the hospital. 'I'd ask you to come, but I know you don't like water.'

There it was — his involvement with this girl Susie — out in the open. 'Thanks, but no, thanks,' she said, and tried to put a smile in her voice.

'Perhaps if you tried it?'

Was he criticising her?

'I have tomorrow planned,' she explained. It sounded like the excuse it was, but she did not care. She was too miserable.

'Perhaps I can persuade you another time?'

'Perhaps.' She only agreed to stop him persisting, but she wished she had been more positive about refusing when he said,

'I'll hold you to that,' turning into the hospital car park.

He waited until she was in her car before he drove away, wondering what had wrought the change in her.

Claire did not turn on the engine, she just sat. But the numbness she had been feeling since Luigi had asked Mark about Susie left her with Mark's going. In its place an agony of emptiness seemed to consume her as she admitted that she was in love with Mark. The sterile world she had been living in was nothing to this. Her happiness lay with this man, and he was already taken.

CHAPTER EIGHT

OVER the next two weeks Claire avoided Mark as much as possible. The children admitted following the coach crash had all gone home. She had received a letter from Steven in which he complained that he had not been able to reach her on the phone.

I'm going to the South of France, but will call again when I get back. I'm serious about you, Claire, and I know you'll forgive me for being precipitate.

His letter filled Claire with annoyance. The arrogance of the man. She had forgiven his aberration and was more cross with herself. She should have put him in his place there and then, and probably would have done if she had not been so upset about Mark. She was further annoyed that she had told Mark about Steven.

Jessie Watson was on a week's holiday, leaving Claire in charge. She was in the office checking the case-notes to make sure they were up to date and that all the reports had been included when there was a knock on the door. A redheaded girl with a cheerful smile popped round the door at Claire's 'Come in.'

'Hello. I'm Hazel. . .' The young woman stopped in mid-sentence. 'Aren't you Claire Forrest?' she said as she came right in.

'Yes.' Claire frowned, then her face cleared. 'Hazel—Hazel Parker,' she said, her eyes lighting with pleasure. And memories of a miniature edition of the young woman standing before her flooded into her mind.

Hazel had been her friend when Claire had stayed for those halcyon holidays at Whiteleigh. There had been an instant rapport between the children, but Hazel's father was in the army and the family had moved from Whiteleigh to Germany when the girls were about ten, and the contact was lost.

'What are you doing here?' Claire asked.

Hazel smiled. 'I might ask you the same question.'

'I'm staffing here for the time being. I'm an agency nurse. Sister Watson's on holiday, so I'm in charge. I always loved it here in Whiteleigh, so I've come back to stay.'

'Well!' Hazel's smile broadened. 'I live here too. I'm a primary school teacher and I've come to see one of my pupils, Kerry Laggat. I thought I could give her some school work so that she won't get too far behind.' Hazel's eyes, the colour of her name, softened. 'She has trouble keeping up as it is,' she confided. 'And as the schools have gone back, the headmistress thought it would be a good idea if I came along.'

Kerry Laggat had been admitted four days ago with concussion and a fractured femur, having been knocked from her cycle by a car.

'Some car drivers aren't aware of cyclists as much as they should be.' Hazel's cheerful face became solemn, then she smiled and produced a large card from her bag. 'The class have sent Kerry this card, signed by them all.'

'Kerry'll love that. We're hoping to discharge her soon, but Mr Stanger's concerned about the headaches she's still having, so he wants to keep her for a bit longer.' They were monitoring Kerry's blood-pressure and pulse, but Claire did not tell Hazel that. 'I'll take you to see her, but she isn't ready for schoolwork yet.' Claire was delighted to see Hazel and grinned at her. 'Kerry's parents aren't with her, as her mother has young children at home and can only come in the afternoon if she can get a babysitter. Her father comes in after his work, or minds the children to let his wife visit.'

They went into the ward. 'I expect she'll be pleased to see you,' said Claire.

Kerry was in bed. She was a small-boned child who did not look as healthy as an eleven-year-old should. There was a slightly anxious expression on her heart-shaped face. Her short curly brown hair was cut close to her scalp, making her head appear smaller, and the slenderness of her body made little impression beneath the bedclothes. Apprehension gripped Claire. Something was wrong. The child was too quiet.

'Hi, Kerry!' Hazel smiled at her pupil.

An irritable frown drew the brown brows together.

'Go away,' said Kerry, her hand waving in a dismissive gesture, but it was said in a dull-eyed, lethargic way.

'When you're better, I'll bring you some school work to do,' said Hazel cheerfully, ignoring Kerry's dismissal. 'Then you won't fall too far behind.'

'Go away!' Kerry's voice rose and tears filled her eyes. 'I'm going to be sick!' she wailed.

Claire tipped sweets out of a bowl on the locker and, raising Kerry's head, slipped it under the child's chin. Tears mixed with the acrid-sweet vomit.

Afterwards, the child lay back exhausted. 'I want my mummy,' she whimpered.

Claire bathed the pale face with a cloth taken from Kerry's sponge bag. 'She'll be here soon, darling,' she said in a soothing tone.

Hazel was still there, and Claire moved to join her at the foot of the bed.

'Don't leave me!' wailed Kerry.

'I won't,' Claire reassured her. 'I just want to speak to Miss Parker.' She turned to Hazel. 'I hate to ask this, but I'm the only one here at the moment — the rest of the staff are at lunch.' She tried to keep the worry she was feeling out of her eyes. 'Would you phone the switchboard and ask them to put you through to Ronnie North—he's our houseman? Tell him to come at once.' Her tone, though low, was urgent. 'Tell him it's an emergency.'

'Right,' said Hazel, her eyes wide. 'And I'll come back afterwards in case I can help.'

'Thanks,' Claire was grateful.

Hazel sped away, her shoes tap-tapping on the wooden floor.

Claire took Kerry's blood-pressure, pulse and respirations and recorded them on the chart. Her anxiety increased when she found Kerry's blood-pressure was raised and her pulse and respirations were lowered.

The ward doors thub-thubbed and Claire glanced eagerly towards them. She hoped to see Ronnie North, but it was Mark Stanger who came striding towards her.

'Am I glad to see you!' she told him in a low voice that only he could hear, relief smoothing the anxious lines from her face.

One glance at the child was enough for Mark. He did not need to query her words. He took the charts she was holding out to him and said quietly,

'That's a change. I thought you'd been avoiding me.'

The amusement in his eyes was fleeting. He directed his attention to the child and sat down on the bed, taking Kerry's hand into his.

As Claire looked at him holding the small hand in his large one, the warmth of her love filled the emptiness of her heart. His kind face, his gentleness, his patience broke down the barrier she had erected, and it did not matter that he was, perhaps, another's. Her feelings could no longer be denied. She loved him—loved him—loved him. Bittersweet it might be, but there was nothing she could do about it. And somehow it was a relief.

'Well, little one,' said Mark, a gentle smile on his face, 'I think we'll have to take you for a little ride.'

'Where to?' The small face became pinched with fear.

'Oh, just down the corridor to a secret room,' said Mark conspiratorially.

But there was no interest in Kerry's face. 'I'm sleepy.'

Ronnie North's large feet thumped down the ward. The staff always knew when he was coming and had nicknamed him 'Tiptoes'. 'No need for the cavalry?' he said, grinning.

Mark raised an eyebrow in disapproval. Kerry's condition was too serious for facetiousness. Ronnie's face straightened immediately. 'Sorry,' he said.

Mark rose and joined Claire and Ronnie at the foot of the bed. 'I think she's had a subdural haematoma. We'll have to evacuate it through a burrhole.' He looked down at the child, whose eyes were closed. 'I knew something was wrong.' He glanced at Claire. 'Phone the parents and tell them what we suspect — ask their permission to operate. I'll inform the theatre and send someone for Kerry.' He took another look at the child, his face creasing with concern. 'She's lapsing into unconsciousness. We'll have to be quick.' He hurried away with a sobered Ronnie.

Hazel passed them on her way back to Claire.

'Can I help?' she asked.

'Yes. Would you nip over to the ward opposite and ask Nurse Andrews to come here, please? I want her to phone Mrs Laggat to tell her that Kerry needs an immediate operation. We have to get her permission.'

Hazel nodded and left Claire taking Kerry's pulse. The theatre staff arrived, and Kerry was away before Hazel had returned.

'I'll bring the permission up when the nurses return from lunch,' Claire promised. 'I'm hoping Mrs Laggat will come straight in.' She held the ward door open for them.

Hazel was replacing the receiver when Claire came into the office. 'Where's Nurse Andrews?' she asked, a worried frown lining her brow.

'She was the only one on the ward and couldn't leave a patient. She said she'd come in a minute, but I knew Kerry's home number — I've had to phone her mother on occasions. . .' Then, seeing the look of horror on Claire's face, Hazel said with anxious eyes, 'Shouldn't I have phoned?' Her pale face became paler. 'I thought it was an emergency?'

Before Claire could reply, Nurse Andrews burst into the office. 'Sorry I couldn't come right away, but the others were at lunch and they've only just come back.' She looked from Claire to Hazel. 'Everything all right?'

Claire did not know Shirley Andrews, but she had heard that the dark-haired nurse was a gossip, so she said, keeping a control on her face,

'Yes, thanks.' Then, seeing Shirley's reluctance to leave, she said, 'You must be ready for your lunch.'

It was a dismissal, and Shirley went. As the door closed behind the nurse, Claire turned to Hazel, whose agitation had increased.

'Thanks for phoning,' she said calmly, hoping to allay her friend's anxiety. 'It's just that you're not a member of the staff.' Then she asked the question she had been eager to know the answer to, 'What did Mrs Laggat say?'

'Just that she'd tell her husband and that he'd be along.'

'Did she give her permission for the operation, though?'

'She said she'd have to ask him,' said Hazel, her anxiety unabated, and it was not relieved at all when Claire moaned,

'Oh!' in an apprehensive manner, as she reached for the phone and dialled the theatre.

When it was answered, she said, 'Tell Mr Stanger that we haven't written permission for the operation on Kerry Laggat. We haven't even got verbal permission.'

A few moments later the nurse was back on the line.

'Mr Stanger says to get it when the parents arrive. He's already operating.'

The answer alleviated Claire's apprehension only a little, as she replaced the receiver. What if the child died?

'I'm sorry if I've got you into trouble,' said Hazel, Claire's anxiety mirrored on her face.

'It's not your fault,' Claire tried to reassure her. 'It's just——'

She did not have time to complete the sentence. A man of medium height and heavily built burst into the office.

'What's all this about operating on my daughter?' It was Mr Laggat. 'I haven't given my permission. She was all right when I saw her last evening. You medical people are always taking things into your own hands.' His face was red as he paused for breath. And then he saw Hazel. 'What's she doing here? She's not a nurse. What right has she to phone my wife and upset her by telling her Kerry has to have an emergency operation?' His face became redder with anger. 'I had to leave my job to come up here and find out what's going on. Fine way to run a hospital. I want to see your boss.' His face was so close to Claire's that she could feel his warm breath on her cheek.

'I didn't want her to stay in. We could have looked after her at home, but the doctor persuaded me to leave her with you lot a bit longer. It's been very inconvenient for us, what with the other children so young.'

Claire was horrified at how a chain of circumstances could escalate out of all proportion. She caught a glimpse of Hazel's stricken face behind the angry man, but before she could speak, the two nurses who had gone to lunch arrived at the doorway, unaware of the trouble their absence had caused. Their appearance halted Mr Laggat's tirade for a moment.

Claire moistened dry lips. 'Would you see if the children in the ward are all right? I'm occupied with Kerry's father for the moment. You'll find she's not in the ward.' There was a sharp intake of breath from the father. 'I'll tell you about it later.'

The nurses, aware of the tension in the office, made no comment, just closed the door, glad to escape.

'You have no right to take my daughter to Theatre without my permission.' Mr Laggat's face was white with fury. 'I didn't know she was already there.'

'Won't you sit down, Mr Laggat?' Claire gestured to the spare chair.

'No,' he answered stiffly. 'What I want is an explanation.' His eyes were fierce, his stance threatening, but Claire detected the anxiety behind the blustering and made allowances for it.

She glanced at Hazel. 'Thanks for your help,' she said quietly. It was a dismissal, and Hazel opened the door, preparing to go.

'I want her to stay.' Mr Laggat barked.

'Very well,' said Claire, and Hazel closed the door.

'Kerry has developed signs of a subdural haematoma,' Claire explained, then hurried on before Mr Laggat could say he did not understand, to tell him in simpler terms what that meant. 'The bang on her head caused the delicate veins to be torn, and blood seeped into a space.'

She paused. Mr Laggat looked as if he did not understand, so she went on, 'The collection of this blood presented symptoms that needed immediate surgery. Kerry was kept in, in case these symptoms occurred.'

Mr Laggat's face paled and he sat down abruptly.

'He didn't tell me something like this might happen.' The anger was still in his voice.

'He wouldn't want to worry you unnecessarily.' Claire spoke quietly. 'It might not have happened. We've been observing your little girl very carefully, and this afternoon she showed the signs I've just mentioned.' Her tone was gentle as she said, 'Kerry was taken to theatre immediately, and the X-ray confirmed Mr Stanger's diagnosis. He's operating now to drain the blood away.'

'I don't really understand what you're saying, but I suppose I'll have to take your word for it.' He sounded drained.

Claire had drawn the permission for operation forward and was inserting Kerry's name.

'What's that for?' Mr Laggat was on his feet, immediately suspicious.

'It's the permission for operation form,' Claire told him firmly. 'I'd like you to sign it.'

'And if I don't, you'll get into trouble.' He sounded as if that was just what he wanted.

She tried to make allowances for Mr Laggat's stress, but she was annoyed by his tone, and said,

'Mr Laggat, Kerry's life was in danger. . .' She thought she heard him gasp. He apparently had not realised how serious his daughter's condition had been. 'Mr Stanger *had* to operate immediately' Then she added more gently, 'I'm sure you would agree to that,' and she pushed the form nearer to him and handed him her pen. He signed without further argument.

Then he saw Hazel. 'But I don't see why a qualified nurse couldn't have phoned my wife instead of this schoolteacher.' He was becoming argumentative again.

So Claire explained, but Mr Laggat seemed determined not to accept her explanation. 'I shall complain to the matron,' he said. 'I'm going home now to comfort my wife, but I'll be back directly.' His tone was hostile once more.

As the door closed behind him Claire sank into his vacated seat.

'I'm sorry if I got you into trouble,' Hazel said guiltily.

'It's not your fault,' Claire comforted her friend. She could not blame Hazel for acting out of kindness. She opened the office door. 'I'd better go and see that everything's ready for Kerry's return.

Hazel paused in the corridor. 'You know, I can't get over the change in Mr Laggat,' she said. Her eyes were bewildered.

'I know.' Claire's face had lost its stressed look. 'I think it was caused by worry. It came out as anger. I've seen it before.'

Hazel sighed. 'How about meeting for coffee some time?' she suggested.

'I'd like that,' said Claire, and meant it.

Hazel drew a notebook out of her bag and took down Claire's number. 'I'll give you a ring,' she promised.

It was with some trepidation that Claire waited for Mr Laggat's return. When he did appear, his wife was with him, and she said, 'I'm sorry for all the fuss, Staff.'

'Don't you apologise,' her husband said sharply.

Mrs Laggat was a small-boned women, five foot two in height, with Kerry's brown hair and a tired, stressed face.

'Why not?' Mrs Laggat straightened her aching back. 'You should be grateful for all the nurses and doctors have done. Kerry would have died if they hadn't been so careful.' She had grasped the situation more fully than her husband, who looked stunned.

Mrs Laggat turned to Claire. 'He's just upset,' she excused her husband. 'He isn't an angry man normally.'

She put her arm through her husband's and looked up at him fondly. 'He loves us all.'

Mr Laggat's face softened as he smiled down at his wife.

'I'm sorry, Staff,' he said to Claire. 'The wife's right.'

He was once again the pleasant man she remembered, and Claire was relieved. She included Mrs Laggat in her smile as she said, 'I'll take you to the waiting-room and one of the nurses will bring you a cup of tea.'

After she had settled the couple, Claire should have gone to lunch, but she wanted to wait for Kerry's return. She phoned the SNO and asked for a nurse to special the child.

'I'll see what I can do, Staff,' said Mrs Godfrey, 'but I won't be able to send you anybody for a while.'

Claire rang off and went into the ward to check on the children. A mother whose child had had its appendix removed two days earlier asked about Kerry in an anxious voice.

'She's in Theatre now, Mrs Standing.' Claire gave her a reassuring smile. She glanced up at the ward clock. 'She should be back any moment now.'

Her words were prophetic, for the ward door opened and the trolley came through with their small patient.

Claire joined the nurse. 'How is she?' She kept her voice low.

'She'll be all right.' The nurse handed Claire the notes. 'But Mr Stanger wants her specialled.' It was the nurse Claire had had to speak firmly to during the emergency. She did not like the girl's arrogant manner now.

'That goes without saying,' Claire said coldly. 'Everything's ready here.'

The nurse raised an insolent eyebrow. 'It better be. Mr Stanger said he'd be down directly.'

She left before Claire could answer. This is definitely

not my day, thought Claire. All I need is for Mark to find fault. So she checked everything again. The relevant charts were recorded accurately, and Kerry's condition was stable.

Claire stroked the pale face, then glanced up and saw Mr and Mrs Laggat's faces framed in the square porthole of the ward door.

She could not leave Kerry, so she attracted the attention of an auxiliary. 'Tell Mr and Mrs Laggat that their daughter is fine and that Mr Stanger will be down soon and will see them.'

Before the woman could carry out Claire's request, Mark's face joined the Laggats'. The door opened and he strode into the ward.

Claire's breath caught in her throat. He was so clean and upright, handsome and distinguished. His grey suit fitted him perfectly; his white shirt was spotless and his tie knotted tightly; Claire did not like loosely tied ties. Everything about him spoke of authority and assurance. He looked as fresh as if he had stepped from his bed instead of a hot operating theatre.

Then her heart missed a beat, but it wasn't because of how he was affecting her. It was the severity of his expression that caused her pulse to quicken.

She handed him the charts, which he took without a word. Then, after he had studied them and checked Kerry for himself, he said, 'I'd like a word with you in the office, Staff.'

'I can't leave Kerry,' Claire told him, her calm face hiding her increasing anxiety. 'The SNO hasn't sent a nurse to special her yet.'

'I'm sure it will be all right to leave an experienced nurse like Mrs James to watch over Kerry for a few minutes. At least she is a nurse and not a schoolteacher.' The blue of his eyes was ice-cold, and Claire had to fight to stop herself shivering.

She was dismayed, but she spoke up boldly. 'I'll be

with you in a moment,' she said, her voice as cold as his.

A flash of white caught Claire's eyes as a nurse she did not know approached them. 'I'm Nurse Conway. The SNO sent me to special a patient of yours.' She did not appear to notice the tension between the staff nurse and the doctor.

'I'll wait for you in the office,' said Mark, giving the nurse a perfunctory smile.

Claire nodded. The handover was completed more quickly than she would have wished, and she could not delay her confrontation with Mark any longer.

He was standing with his back towards her as she entered the office, but he swung round as she closed the door. Her mouth went dry with apprehension.

'I was shocked to hear that you asked a primary school teacher to phone Mrs Laggat about Kerry.' His face was stiff with controlled anger. 'It was not only a breach of confidentiality, but it could have had misleading effects. Miss Parker, in her ignorance, might have given the wrong message.' His tone softened a little as he continued, 'Though apparently she was very pleasant and sympathetic.' Then his face hardened again. 'But what I can't understand is how an experienced nurse like yourself could have asked her to phone in the first place.'

Claire decided to tell him the truth, but in such a way as to absolve Hazel. So, straightening her back and taking a deep breath, she looked him in the eyes and said,

'I really think you're making a little too much out of this.' His face became sterner at what he considered an insolent reply. Claire did not even notice his resemblance to the man in her dream, she just saw his anger, but she went on, unafraid, 'You weren't here, so how could you know what the situation was? I was on my own as the rest of the staff were at lunch, and I couldn't

leave Kerry.' The anxiety caused by the events of the
morning, coupled with his attitude, made her angry.
'Even you wouldn't have countenanced that. So I did
the only thing possible. I asked Hazel Parker. . .' she
looked at him coldly as she said it, '. . .a person I know
to be as competent as any nurse and someone the
family were familiar with to phone Mrs Laggat and ask
for her permission to operate.' She paused for breath.
Mark's face had not changed.

'I explained the situation to Mr Laggat, and after he
returned with his wife he accepted it.' Claire's eyes
narrowed. 'Why? Did he complain?'

Mark's face was still stiff, but his voice was not as
cold as he said, 'No. Mrs Laggat let the cat out of the
bag——'

Claire interrupted him angrily, 'I can assure you that
this cat was not hiding in any bag!'

Amusement crept into his eyes. 'All right, all right.'
He dodged backwards, hand upraised. 'No need to
attack me.' He grinned. 'Mrs Laggat was very grateful
to you. It was me who was shocked.'

'That doesn't say much for your confidence in me,'
retorted Claire, unwilling to see his side.

'Now who's quibbling,' he said, but he was smiling,
and it melted her like the sun melted the snow, and she
longed to throw herself into his arms, kiss and make
up, wipe the stress and tiredness of her day away in the
security of his embrace, but all she did was to smile in
return, not realising how her thoughts were imprinted
on her face.

He reached forward and took her into his arms and
kissed her gently on the forehead, the eyelids, the
cheeks until, finally, his lips touched her soft mouth.

He could feel his passion mounting, and the effort to
subdue it made his face flush.

Claire felt as if she were in a land of warmth and
sunlight, of pale blue skies which stretched on forever.

It would be so lovely to stay in this land and not to
have to come back to the reality that for Mark this was
not the whole of his existence, that to him they were
just kisses, for if he felt more he would—

A knock at the door broke them apart. Mrs James
came in.

'Staff Nurse Conway would like to see you—'

There was no need for her to say more, as both Mark
and Claire rushed to Kerry's bedside. It was a surprised
staff nurse who greeted them with,

'Well, I call that service. I only wanted to know how
long I'm to take Kerry's blood-pressure—quarter-
hourly?'

Claire and Mark looked at each other and laughed.
The tensions of the day slipped away from their faces,
as Mark looked at the chart an amused Staff Nurse
Conway had given him.

'We'd better go cautiously with her,' he said. 'We
don't want a relapse.' He glanced at the staff nurse.
'We'll keep her sedated for now.' He handed back the
charts. 'You can reduce taking her blood-pressure to
half-hourly if it remains constant.'

Claire accompanied Mark out of the ward. He
paused outside the office door. 'Don't hesitate to send
for me—I'll be in the hospital until five.' He smiled
down at her. 'Let Kerry's parents go in and see her,
but there's no point in their staying when she's sedated.
Tell them to come back later.'

And with that he turned and left her without a word
to show that the interlude in the office had meaning for
him.

Sadness tugged at Claire repeatedly for the rest of
her duty, but by the time she left the hospital at six she
had resolved to stop moping. So she was in love with
Mark Stanger—but was she? Perhaps it was just infatu-
ation. After all, he was the first man she had been

attracted to, and maybe the face in the dream had influenced her.

Claire deliberately suppressed the memory of Mark's lips touching her eyes, her cheeks, her lips. Memories. . . She braked the car just in time — the lights had changed to red. The fright jolted all thoughts of Mark from her mind.

Having parked the car, Claire was waiting for the lift when the doors glided back smoothly and Mark with Susie on his arm stepped out. There was no way that Claire could avoid them.

Mark's face was expressionless as he introduced the girl. 'This is Claire Forrest, the staff nurse on the children's ward at Whiteleigh General.' His eyes were unreadable as he said, 'This is Susie Collins.'

Claire smiled at Susie. Only one side of the girl's face was scarred, the untouched one was beautiful, but there was a guarded look in the blue eyes.

'I hear you sail,' said Claire naturally.

The scarring of Susie's face puckered as she smiled, distorting her features, but Claire's expression did not alter.

'Yes,' said Susie enthusiastically. 'Mark takes me on his boat. Do you sail?'

'No.' Claire could not prevent her body from stiffening, nor keep the tightness out of her voice. 'I'm afraid of the sea,' she confessed.

'I can understand that,' said Susie sympathetically.

Claire was grateful. So many people scoffed when she told them, so she did not usually mention it.

'We all have some form of disfigurement, don't we?' said Susie, smiling, and Claire was impressed.

The rapport between the two young women had excluded Mark, but now he said, 'Come along, Susie. We must get you up to London.'

But Susie lingered. 'I'm starting a series of operations tomorrow,' she told Claire, who heard the underlying vulnerability.

Her face softened and she put an arm round the girl's shoulders. 'I hope everything goes well with you,' she murmured, giving Susie a hug.

'I wish you were going to nurse me.' Susie's voice was wistful.

'Perhaps we can do something about that,' said Mark, looking directly at Claire. 'Will you be free when Sister Watson returns from holiday?'

There was nothing else for Claire to say except, 'Well, I suppose so. Staff Nurse Rogers, the ward staff nurse, is coming back.'

'Well, please hold yourself available.' It was Mark Stanger, the ward consultant, speaking.

Was this the man who had kissed her so recently? He sounded so distant. But then he had not had Susie on his arm. Susie was his girlfriend, not herself.

'Very well, Doctor,' Claire said with equal stiffness, but she smiled at her prospective patient and said, 'I'll look forward to seeing you soon, then, Susie.'

It was only when Claire was in the lift that she realised the position she had placed herself in. She had committed herself to nursing Mark's young lady back to her full beauty.

Tragedy met Claire when she reported for duty next morning. Kerry Laggat had relapsed during the night and had died in the small hours.

Claire knew something had happened as soon as she entered the office. There was a subdued atmosphere, and the night nurse's eyes were red. They filled with tears again as she gave the report.

'It happened so suddenly.' There was a catch in her voice.

Claire laid a hand on the night nurse's shoulder.

'Look, give us the rest of the report, then you can

tell me all about it over a cup of tea.' Her own eyes smarted. The death of a child was even more harrowing than the death of an adult.

When the day nurses had left, and a cup of tea was before the night nurse, Claire said, 'Tell me,' in her gentlest voice.

'It was about two o'clock. Nurse Reilly, who was specialling Kerry, rang the bell. When I arrived at the bedside, she said, "Get the doctor quickly." I didn't ask why, I just flew to the office and phoned for Ronnie. I thought he'd never come, but when he did, he had Mr Stanger with him.' A dreamy look came into the nurse's eyes. 'Even at two o'clock in the morning that man looks gorgeous. I think his stubble added to his attraction.' She sighed. 'I wonder if he sleeps in the buff.'

Visions of Mark rising naked from his bed had to be suppressed, so Claire said sharply, to bring the night nurse and herself back to the report, 'And. . .?'

The nurse's face, which had brightened at thoughts of the handsome consultant, became sad once more. 'They rushed her to Theatre, but it was too late. She died before they could even put her on the table.' Tears darkened the smudges beneath the night nurse's eyes. 'The parents are devastated, particularly the father. He was ranting at Mr Stanger, accusing him of operating unnecessarily, and saying he hadn't given his permission.'

The nurse reached for Kerry's notes and flicking them open drew out the signed consent form. 'But here it is,' she looked up at Claire with a bewildered frown.

'Yes.' Claire did not enlighten the girl, she just thanked her. 'You go off to bed and get some sleep.'

The young woman, in her early twenties, smiled and said. 'Oh, I will. I could sleep for a week.'

When she had left, Claire opened Kerry's notes and

saw written in Mark's strong handwriting, "Died at two-thirty a.m."

Tears gathered in her eyes. The words were so final. 'What a waste,' she said out loud, and the tears for what Kerry might have been fell on to the page, making a large full stop after the word.

Hastily she dried it and closed the folder, shivering a little. This was the last chapter of Kerry's life.

'I see you know.'

Claire had been so involved with her thoughts that she had not heard Mark come in. She swung round, and was shocked at the ravages she saw on his face. It looked older, more like the face in her dream, but that did not disturb her. It was the despair she saw in his blue eyes that shook her. She had thought he was such a self-contained man, thought that nothing could disturb his equanimity. To know that he suffered like everyone else broke down another barrier between them, one she had not realised existed until then. It was not that she had thought him unfeeling. It was just that her own uncertainty in life had led her to believe that this big, strong man, full of confidence, could never be shaken by anything. What a lot she had to learn about him, and if only she could be with him all the time to do just that—but there *was* something she could do.

'Sit down,' she said, in a firm voice.

He closed the door and did as she bade, and this more than anything stirred her compassion. 'You mustn't blame yourself. There was nothing you could do.'

'Wasn't there?' He was like one of the children—wanting reassurance, his eyes full of pain.

Claire knelt down before him, not feeling the hardness of the floor beneath her knees. Her face was almost level with his. She took both his cold hands in hers and clasped them tightly.

'Look at me,' she ordered, and held his eyes with hers as he did so.

She knew, from past experience, that she had an almost uncanny power to hypnotise. It was something that frightened her, and she had hardly ever used it. It had manifested itself when she was a young child and had followed the trauma that had left her with the dream.

Now she was happy she had this gift, for it meant she could help Mark. And this she did, murmuring in soft tones, convincing him that he had done all that he could to save Kerry.

Mark felt, as he gazed into her blue eyes, that he was looking into a clear bottomless pool, and that her gentle voice was drawing him deeper and deeper into it. A feeling of peace which he had never experienced before filled his whole being. All his doubts vanished and he felt whole again, knowing that he *had* done his best. He felt renewed.

He smiled, then his smile turned to concern, for Claire looked exhausted. 'Are you all right?' he demanded. Even his voice had recovered its firmness.

'Yes.' And she did appear to be. Her colour was returning, now that she did not need to exert such force.

'Thank you for your help,' Mark said softly, not quite knowing what she had done to lift his despair, but knowing that she had.

'I'm glad you're feeling better,' she said, her voice deep with sincerity, her smile enigmatic.

Before he could ask her what she had done to help him, the office door burst open without a knock.

'There you are.' It was Mr Laggat. 'I'm going to sue you both.'

'No, you're not.' Mark had risen to his full height. He made an imposing figure, head and shoulders above the smaller man. The ravages had left his face. His eyes were alert and compelling, almost as compelling as Claire's had been a moment earlier.

Mr Laggat's mouth gaped. Then his face became pinched, his red cheeks paled, and he sank into Mark's vacated seat, his shoulders bowed.

Claire was so sorry for him. She said, 'I know there's nothing anybody can say that will help, but the doctor did his best, believe me.'

The grief in his eyes was appalling, and she felt helpless. She could not take his burden from him as she had Mark's.

The sorrowing man rose slowly to his feet. 'I'm sorry.' His whispered apology was worse than his blustering.

Claire put an arm round his bowed shoulders. 'I'll get you a cup of tea,' she murmured.

'No, thanks. I'd better go home.'

'I'll run you,' Mark offered, and the stricken man did not refuse.

After they had left Claire sank into the chair, but she had work to do, and she rose after a moment and went into the ward. There were others to attend to.

CHAPTER NINE

OVER the next few weeks the bond between Claire and Susie grew. Claire admired the younger woman's courage, for, even when in pain, Susie did not complain. These must be the qualities that had drawn Mark to the younger woman and not the hope of her beauty being restored — that was just a bonus.

This knowledge added to Claire's misery. What must Mark think of me, with my fear of the sea? Does he despise me? she wondered. He certainly had not given her any reason to suppose that his feelings were as deep as hers. It was agony seeing him every day. She dreaded his visits and yet longed for them.

Mark was there when the final bandages were removed. He was holding Susie's hand as Claire removed the dressings. She could feel his eyes upon her, but Claire was looking into Susie's fearful ones.

Claire's face was as tense as the atmosphere in the room as the last layer came away. Then it relaxed into a wide smile.

'Take a look,' she said, handing Susie the mirror.

Tentatively the young woman accepted it, but did not immediately look into the glass; her eyes were still on Claire.

'Is it all right?' she whispered anxiously.

'Yes, it is. Really it is,' Claire encouraged her gently.

Susie looked into the mirror and tears gleamed in her eyes. 'It's true. My face has been restored.' She glanced up at Mark and said something that seemed strange to Claire. 'Thank you for all you've done.'

Mark stooped and gave her a hug. 'Think nothing of it.'

126

Claire moved the dressings trolley towards the door. She felt in the way and was eager to escape. She had just reached the treatment-room when Mark caught up with her and held the door open.

'I want to thank you for all you've done for Susie.' His face was serious.

Claire noted the dark rings below his eyes and knew how travelling to see Susie each day had exacted a toll.

'You don't need to thank me,' she said with a smile. 'It was a pleasure. You're very lucky—Susie's a delightful girl.' Her eyes could not hide her misery, and Mark suddenly realised what was wrong. Claire thought that he and Susie were lovers.

He grinned. 'Yes, she is, and now she's free.'

Claire looked puzzled. 'Free?'

His grin broadened. 'Free of any stigma. Free to do as she pleases. Free to find a boyfriend of her own age.' He touched Claire's cheek gently. 'I only helped to boost her confidence. There's nothing like being seen in the company of an attractive man to make you feel good.' It wasn't said out of conceit.

Claire was so overcome by emotion that she could not reply immediately and busied herself disposing of the dirty dressing bag.

A strong hand took hold of her arm and she was pulled swiftly into his embrace. A kiss such as she had never dreamed of swept her literally off her feet. When Mark set her down again, her hair was awry, her dress rumpled, her face flushed.

'There,' he said with a grin, 'I've been wanting to do that for a long time.'

'Why didn't you?' she surprised herself by saying, looking up at him coquettishly.

Mark was delighted at her response. He still had his arms round her. 'I intend to make up for lost time,' he told her, his voice rough with desire.

'Is that a threat?' she joked in a whisper.

'No, a promise.' And he kissed her, but gently.

'I don't think much of that,' she said with a smile, and, reaching up, she kissed *him*, her arms going round his neck to keep him close. He could feel her trembling, even as his desire mounted and restrained himself. He did not want to frighten her, and in any case, the treatment-room was not the place to make love.

He put her from him with a smile. 'How about dinner this evening?' he said.

'I'd love to.' Her heart was in her eyes, and Mark was thrilled. Claire loved him, but he must be careful. Her love was tender and could be killed by a lack of sensitivity, just as the frost killed off the young shoots.

But their dinner was not to be. Mark was called on to perform an emergency operation on a child who had been involved in a serious road accident.

The next day was Friday and Claire was returning to Whiteleigh. Mark was operating all day, but he did manage to meet her for lunch in the hospital canteen.

'I'll be down late this evening,' he told her. His eyes held hers, and she read in them what she had longed to see — love — love for her. She found it hard to believe, and wondered if she had just imagined it. For how could someone like Mark love her — tangled up as she was? Surely it must show — her doubts about herself, the underlying anxiety that the dream might recur. She would have to tell him about the dream, but she did not want to spoil their developing relationship.

He saw how troubled she was and thought she was worrying about her lack of experience in the art of love. He smiled and reached for her hand, oblivious to the interest this caused amongst the rest of the diners.

'Don't look so worried, darling,' he said, smiling. 'There's nothing to be afraid of. You'll be safe with me. I'll not harm you.'

Safe with him. What wonderful words. But would he be safe with her? What about the dream?

Claire managed to smile, knowing that he had spoken to calm any anxieties she might have about their sexual relationship. Nothing formal had been said between them, but they both knew that eventually they would be together.

She pushed unwelcome thoughts aside and really smiled this time.

'Must go,' said Mark, rising. 'See you at the weekend.'

Claire had arranged to meet Hazel on Saturday morning, something she had forgotten to tell Mark. She would phone her and explain that something had come up. Her relationship with Mark was too new to tell anybody about. Claire wanted to hug it to herself, and she did not want to miss a minute of the time with him.

She was dressing in jeans and a jumper when the bell rang. Expecting a parcel, she thought it must be the postman, but it was Steven who greeted her with,

'Hello, pet.'

Claire had forgotten all about him. She had not heard from him, and thought he had realised that he was not in love with her.

'Hello, Steven,' she said.

His smiling face was just the same, she could almost imagine that his attempt at lovemaking had not happened, but the words he had spoken were still with her and her greeting was stiff.

'Aren't you going to invite me in?' There was a trace of impatience in his tone.

Reluctantly, she opened the door wider. 'I'm going out, so you can only stay a minute.' Her manner was offhand.

Steven glanced at his watch. 'Just time for a cup of coffee, then.' His attractive face broke into a smile.

So many memories, so many years could not be brushed aside, so she said, 'Come into the kitchen.'

Steven waited until she had pushed a mug of coffee in front of him, then he said, 'I'm awfully sorry I scared you the last time I was here. Can you forgive me?' His face wore his little boy's pleading look, one she was well used to.

'Consider it forgotten,' she said with a smile.

'I was too quick with you, Claire, and I'm sorry.' His face became tight. 'But I won't let that man have you.' He took a step nearer to her, so near that she could smell his aftershave; it was a brand she disliked.

'Really, Steven.' She was exasperated. 'I don't love you, and you don't love me.' She suddenly had an idea of how she could convince him. 'Anyway, you're too late.'

'What do you mean?' His voice was sharp.

'Come to dinner this evening and I'll tell you.' She was pushing him out of the front door as she spoke.

He resisted her. 'Tell me now.'

'I haven't time,' she said. 'I'm meeting a friend and should have been there now,' which wasn't strictly true.

'But——'

Claire closed the door on his bewildered face, half expecting him to hammer on it, but there was no sound.

What a good job I didn't phone Hazel, she thought, dialling Mark's number. I'll invite her as well. There was no reply. She'd have to ring him later; he was vital to her plan.

Snatching up her beige leather jacket and bag, she hurried from the flat.

Hazel was waiting for her inside the Copper Kettle where they had arranged to meet.

'Sorry I'm late,' said Claire, taking the seat opposite her friend, 'but Steven held me up.'

'Steven?' Hazel's eyes became interested. 'How is he?'

Copper ornaments on the shelves, copper plaques on the walls, glowed the colour of Hazel's hair. The café was as cheerful as Hazel was herself.

'He's fine,' said Claire. 'Would you like to come to dinner this evening and see for yourself?'

Hazel's eyes gleamed. 'I'd love to. I always did have a crush on him, remember?'

Over their coffee they reminisced about their childhood.

'I used to wait for you two to come out, sometimes for hours,' laughed Hazel, 'and tag along behind you.' Her cheerful smile was the same as it had been when she was a child, thought Claire, envying the clearness of her friend's nature. No secrets there, she mused.

'Do you think he guessed?' There was a wistfulness in Hazel's tone.

'I'm not sure,' said Claire with a smile. 'He never said anything.'

'He was so kind, and never cross,' Hazel smiled. 'Is he just the same?'

Claire did not want to spoil her friend's memories, so she said, 'You'll have to decide for yourself.' She rose. 'Well, if I'm entertaining this evening I'd better get some food.'

Hazel laughed.

'See you at eight,' said Claire as they parted outside the Copper Kettle.

She arrived back later than she intended, and immediately phoned Mark.

'Hello.' His deep voice was so close to her ear, as if at kissing distance, that she was deprived of speech for a moment. Then she said,

'It's Claire. You remember how you said if there was anything you could do. . .?'

'Ye—es,' said Mark, his tone cautious, though she could hear the laughter in his voice.

'Well. . .' She paused. She was a little unsure of him.

'If you're free this evening, will you come to dinner at eight?' she finished in a rush.

'That doesn't seem very difficult to do,' he said with a laugh.

'You haven't heard it all yet.' She smiled, and her smile must have shown in her tone, for he said,

'We—ll?'

'Steven's coming.'

'Ah! Now all is made clear.'

'And Hazel Parker.' Claire had been a little nervous about telling him her friend was also a guest, but he did not comment on that, he just said,

'You want to use me as a buffer to your cousin.' His tone was light.

'I thought a little more than that.' She took a deep breath. 'I thought if he could see. . .' was she being presumptuous. . .? '. . .that you and I. . .' Her courage failed her.

'That you and I are a couple,' Mark finished for her.

'Yes.'

He laughed at the relief he heard in her voice.

'It's my mission in life to help distressed females, especially when they're beautiful and their cousins have designs on them.'

She could hear the amusement in his tone and laughed. 'Then you'll come?'

'With all haste, my darling.' It was spoken softly, seductively.

Oh! she thought. I wish it were eight o'clock.

'Are you there?'

'I wish it was eight o'clock.' She did not mean to speak her thoughts out loud, but her longing for him was so great they just fell from her lips.

Mark gave a low laugh. 'We can remedy that now,' he said.

Claire took hold of herself. 'If we do, there'll be no dinner. I want Steven to realise that he doesn't love me, and I'm hoping that when he sees you and me together, so to speak, he'll lose interest and stop annoying me.'

'I wouldn't,' Mark said so quietly Claire almost did not hear him.

'I wouldn't want you to,' she said as quietly.

'I could be down in a minute. . .' he said eagerly.

She laughed. 'No!' she said firmly.

'Spoilsport.' But he laughed as well. 'See you at eight.'

Claire spent the rest of the day preparing the meal. She wanted it to be perfect and had chosen all the things Steven liked. They would start with pâté, followed by chicken in a wine sauce which she was particularly good at making; it was a recipe of her grandmother's. The dessert would be raspberry Pavlova, and, to follow, a selection of cheeses, with coffee. Rather like the condemned man's last meal, she thought with a shiver.

When she had prepared the meal as far as she could and left the table gleaming with silver and fine china, she went to have her bath.

In the bedroom she slipped the dress she had bought that morning over her head. The midnight-blue made her blue eyes look more intense and her fair skin fairer. The neck was heart-shaped, the bodice draped. It had long sleeves and a straight skirt, and the soft material gave her a sleeping allure. It had been very expensive. Black patent leather shoes completed the outfit.

Claire brushed her hair back and fixed it with combs. The style emphasised her high cheekbones and refined her features even further.

The bell rang, sending her nerves jangling. She opened the front door, and Mark was there. His eyes told her what she knew already, that she looked fantastic.

'I like that,' he said in an exaggerated husky voice.

'You know the old saying—"Good enough to eat"?
Are you sure you're not the main course?'

She burst out laughing. Excitement stirred her, and
she blushed as she saw the look in his eyes.

Mark kicked the front door closed with his foot.
Taking her in his arms, he whispered, 'I wish they
weren't coming.'

Part of Claire wished they weren't as well, but part
of her was worried. Would she freeze when he made
love to her? So she just smiled hesitantly.

Mark smiled gently. His kiss was gentle as well. In
his arms, her doubts faded. She wanted him with all
the power of her body. 'Mark,' she whispered against
his lips. His kiss this time was less gentle and more
passionate,

The doorbell rang. Mark released her, but retained
her hand and opened the door.

Steven's face stiffened and his eyes narrowed as he
saw their flushed faces. It did not take much of a guess
to know what the couple had been doing.

'Ah, Steven.' Mark smiled impudently.

'Have we met?' drawled Steven in an arrogant tone.

'Oh, you've forgotten,' said Mark, raising his eyebrows. 'I *am* disappointed.' His eyes were mocking.

Claire knew Steven very well and saw his anger
rising. She rushed to placate him.

'You remember Mark—he's my ward consultant.' It
was the wrong thing to say, and Steven's face turned
red. 'Shall we have a drink?' She interposed herself
between the two men.

Mark took her arm in a possessive way. 'What a
good idea,' he agreed, and led her into the lounge.

She had just handed Mark a whisky and Steven a gin
when the bell rang again.

'That'll be Hazel,' she said, glad to escape the
tension that was almost a living thing in the room.

'Sorry I'm late,' said the redhead breathlessly. 'But

a friend phoned just as I was leaving, and she's a compulsive talker.' Hazel laughed. She was wearing a green dress that suited her complexion.

'That's all right. Steven's just arrived.' Claire took her friend into the lounge.

The first thing she saw was Steven's face, white with anger. She cast an enquiring glance in Mark's direction. He gave a small shrug, but his eyes were dancing.

Perhaps this idea of hers had not been such a good one, Claire thought apprehensively.

'You remember Hazel?' she said, and was pleased to hear how calm she sounded.

Mark nodded, but Steven frowned.

'I used to follow you around when you came here for your summer holidays,' Hazel explained.

Steven's face relaxed into a charming smile.

'Yes.' He came forward, hand outstretched. 'What are you doing here? I thought your family were in Germany.'

'Fancy you remembering.' Hazel's eyes were full of admiration.

'I always remember redheads,' said Steven suavely. Hazel's reaction was balm to his wounded pride.

Claire saw Mark pull a face behind her cousin's back and felt as if she had let loose a demon.

Steven took Hazel over to the drinks cabinet. Mark sidled up to Claire and whispered close to her ear,

'How am I doing?'

It was impossible not to smile up into his mischievous face. 'I'm not sure,' she said. 'What did you say to Steven when I was at the door?'

'Oh, nothing much.' His tone was airy, but his eyes were twinkling. 'Just that I was going to marry you.'

Claire's jaw dropped.

Pleased with the effect of his words, Mark grinned.

'Well, you wanted to put him off, didn't you? and that was the only effective way I could think of.'

She was speechless. He gave a low laugh and took her arm.

'That's not quite the way I expected my proposal to be received,' he said, the impish look back in his eyes. 'Normally a kiss is given.' Turning her to him, he kissed her lightly on the lips, taking her by surprise.

As he let her go, Claire glanced in her cousin's direction, but he had his back towards her. Hazel, though, was facing them, and her eyes widened. Steven swung round, a frown on his face.

'Just kissing my fiancée,' said Mark blithely.

Claire just managed to prevent her jaw dropping a second time.

'I'll just check on the dinner,' she said, catching Mark's hand and pulling him with her. 'You can help me, darling,' she said sweetly.

She dropped his hand in the kitchen. 'What are you playing at?' she demanded, hurt because their engagement wasn't true.

Mark took hold of both her hands and drew her forward, into his arms. He looked deep into her eyes and said softly,

'I'm not playing. I want you to be my wife.'

Claire searched his face to see if he was telling the truth, and what she saw there filled her with a happiness that she had never known. Mark loved her.

'I was going to wait a little longer before asking you, but. . .' He bent his head and kissed her. 'Why wait when we both know?' he said, releasing her. 'Will you be my wife, the mother of my children?'

Children. What about the dream that had haunted her since her childhood?

'Well?' he queried, not understanding why she hesitated. 'What's your answer?'

She saw the concern in his eyes, the vulnerability behind this concern, and said, 'Yes.' Her face brightening. To hell with the dream, she thought. I love this man and I mean to have him. 'Yes—yes—yes,' she said; each word became softer as she spoke it and her face drew closer to his until her final, 'Yes,' was said with her lips on his.

His arms tightened about her—she could feel the strength in them, and revelled in the moment as she melted against him, soft and yielding. His lips parted hers in a kiss that held almost all his passion, for even though her response thrilled him he managed not to overwhelm her. There would be time. . .

A voice came from the kitchen door. 'We are invited for dinner, I suppose?' It was Steven.

Mark let Claire go reluctantly, but kept his arm round her. 'We became a little sidetracked,' he explained with a grin, not at all apologetic.

'I suppose I should congratulate you,' said Steven, but there was a sarcastic note in his voice and Claire drew closer to Mark, upset by her cousin's tone.

Hazel's appearance just then was welcome. 'Can I have another sherry?' she asked brightly.

'Steven will pour you one,' said Mark, 'while I help Claire dish up the dinner. We'll be with you in a moment or two.'

Steven left, his back stiff with anger. Hazel, who had no idea what it was all about, shrugged and followed him. Claire hoped his mood would not spoil the evening.

But as the meal progressed, her apprehension evaporated. Steven was amusing, and the main reason for the dinner's success. He entertained them with stories of his travels and kept them laughing, leading Claire to suppose he had accepted her engagement.

But as he said, 'Goodnight,' he whispered close to her ear, 'I don't believe in this engagement. Mark's too sophisticated for you. You'll come back to me when he ditches you,' and he hurried to catch up with Hazel.

As she walked back towards the lounge, Claire

wondered if Steven was right. Would Mark find her boring?

'Time for me to go as well, sweetheart,' Mark said with a smile. 'I've a sailing date tomorrow.'

Claire hid her disappointment behind a bright smile. His kiss was long and lingering and left her breathless, sweeping away her doubts. 'I'll call you,' he promised as she saw him out.

On Monday, the agency asked her to return to the children's ward at Whiteleigh General. Staff Nurse Rogers had been rushed to surgery with acute appendicitis.

Mark did not call her that day, or during the next few days, but she both heard and saw Steven. He was waiting for her every time she came off duty, either outside the hospital or the flat.

'How do you know when I'm off duty?' she asked him when this had happened on two occasions.

'Ah, that's my secret,' he laughed. He had phoned the ward and asked one of the staff, but he did not tell Claire that.

'If you think you're wearing me down and that I'll admit you're right about Mark, you're suffering under a delusion,' Claire told him crossly. 'I'm going to marry Mark.'

'Oh?' Steven raised his eyebrows. 'Well, where is he?' he gloated.

She was immediately suspicious. 'How do you know he isn't here?'

Steven was bursting with triumph. 'Because I arranged for him not to be.'

For a moment she was speechless. They were standing on the steps at the hospital entrance. Steven was wearing clothes of impeccable cut. His fair hair was short, his face lightly tanned. There was a strong family resemblance between them. His sports jacket of fine tweed had tiny flecks of blue and grey in the weave, the colours matched his eyes. He was extremely handsome and presentable, but Claire felt nothing for him; even her affection had dimmed.

'What do you mean?' she asked in a whisper.

He took her arm and led her to the car. It was three o'clock on a chilly afternoon. Claire shivered, but not with the cold. It was anxiety that made her tremble. What had Steven done?

She stopped at the car door.

'Get in,' said Steven.

'No!' Claire was adamant. 'Tell me what you've been up to.'

A slight breeze ruffled his hair. He smoothed the stray strands back off his forehead.

'I'd already made enquiries about Mr Stanger.' There was a sneer in his voice. 'Did you know that he's the chief instigator of a rehabilitation unit for children and young adults recovering from burns?'

Claire's expression told him that she didn't, but what her expression did not tell him was how this information explained Mark's interest in Susie. So that was why he had been so attentive to the young scarred girl.

'Well, I donated a sizeable sum of money to this centre, enough for them to build an extension to the existing house — anonymously, of course. Plans have to be approved, committees consulted. . . I'm surprised he hasn't told you.' Steven's eyes were watching her carefully.

So am I, thought Claire.

Steven read her face correctly and said, 'He hasn't phoned you.'

'If he has all those things to do, he's probably been too busy,' said Claire defensively.

'Of course.' There was an underlying mockery in his tone.

She ignored this and opened the car door. She was

behind the wheel, about to close the door, when his hand shot out and grasped it.

She gave him a look of intense dislike and jerked the door out of his hand and slammed it shut. She had the key in the ignition, the engine on and was away before he could collect himself. Claire could see his angry face in the driving mirror and wished he would leave her alone.

A thrill of delight swept through her as she drew in beside Mark's car. He was home. Steven's innuendoes slipped from her mind.

The lift seemed to take ages to come, and, when it did, rose too slowly. She was out before the doors had finished opening and ringing Mark's bell before they had closed.

The door opened and there he was, almost filling the door-frame. The expression on his face made her ashamed of her doubting thoughts. It was full of love.

He swept her into his arms without a word and kissed her gently to begin with, but as his suppressed passion took hold, his lips became more demanding.

Claire responded joyfully, uninhibitedly. There was no frigidity in the way her body reacted. When they broke apart they were both breathless.

'You've been away—you didn't tell me.' She sounded like a child, looked like a child as she gazed up at him for reassurance.

'I didn't think I needed to,' he murmured, his arms still round her. 'When two people love each other, their trust in each other needs no phone calls.'

He was leading her into the lounge as he spoke.

'As it was, I didn't have a free minute, and when I'd finished for the day, it was usually about midnight.' He smiled down at her. 'I didn't want to disturb your beauty sleep.' His smile broadened. 'Now, I want you to meet my father.'

Claire's eyes were on Mark, but a movement from

the couch drew them away. A tall, grey-haired man had risen and was approaching them.

It was then that Claire knew she could never marry Mark, for the man facing her was the man in her dreams, the man who had haunted her all these years, and he was Mark's father.

CHAPTER TEN

IT WAS only by making a supreme effort that Claire
managed not to faint. Her love for Mark and her strong
desire not to hurt him pushed back the dizziness that
threatened. She even made herself take the proffered
hand stretching towards her, stiffening to prevent herself from shivering at its touch.

The face which had filled her with terror was smiling
a smile just like Mark's, but Claire did not see it like
that; to her the smile was a rictus, a death mask.

She hardly heard John Stanger's words of pleasure
at the introduction. She knew she must be smiling, for
her lips were stretched, but she could not speak, her
mouth was too dry, and all she wanted to do was to
leave, escape from this awful presence.

Eventually her mouth became moist enough for her
to say, 'I'm afraid. . .' Unconsciously, she used the
words that described how she was feeling. Then she
said, moving towards the door with a fixed smile on
her face,

'I must leave. . . I have an appointment.' The lie
slipped easily from her tongue.

Mark went with her to the lift. 'Do you have to go
so soon?' His eyes were puzzled. He could not understand her dislike of his father and only hoped he had
not sensed it.

'Yes—I must go.' She knew she sounded feverish,
but she could not help it. She had to go, and now. She
knew she was running away, but she could not help
herself.

'I'm sorry,' she murmured. Would the lift never
come? It took all her self-control to stop herself from

142

fleeing down the stairs, but she could not do that to Mark.

Eventually it arrived, and its coming broke the tension between them. Claire darted in, and the last thing she saw of Mark was his frowning expression.

She avoided Mark for the next two weeks, and she was helped in this by his many absences. Whenever they did meet, he was cheerful and made no reference to his father.

Claire was no longer needed on the children's ward and had accepted work on the general side. She also took some private patients so that she would see less of Mark.

She had just finished relieving the regular nurse who was attending a private patient suffering from muscular dystrophy, and was looking forward to a few days off, when the phone rang. It was the agency.

'I know you've been working flat out for the past week, Claire, but a case has just come in with a special request for you to attend the patient. It's male, aged seventy, with a left-sided hemiplegia. He was admitted to. . .' here the girl named an expensive nursing home in Whiteleigh '. . .yesterday. Will you take the case?'

'Who recommended me?' Claire asked.

There was a pause, then. . .'A Sister Jessie Watson,' came the reply. Claire could hear the rustle of papers in the background.

She would have refused if it had been anyone else but Jessie. She had been living in a nightmare ever since she had found that the man in her dream was Mark's father. Only work kept her sane. Her nights were spent wondering if she was going mad. Did she love Mark? She had heard how people fell in love with their tormentors. Was this, in some crazy way, why she loved him — because he looked so like the man in her dream? She thought more about this than the actual

man himself. She had planned to try and rest for a
couple of days, knowing how exhausted her obsession
with these thoughts was making her, but she could not
refuse Jessie.

'When do you want me to start?' she asked.

'Today, if you can.' There was an apologetic note in
the voice on the other end of the line.

'All right. Tell them I'll report at two o'clock.'

It was only after she had replaced the receiver that
she realised she had not been told the patient's name.

So she was not prepared, and would certainly have
refused the case, when she was taken to the patient's
bedside to discover it was Mark Stanger's father she
had agreed to nurse.

Claire knew, as soon as she saw the still figure lying
in the bed, that Mark had asked Jessie to employ her.
Claire's resentment at this helped her to overcome her
initial repugnance for the man in the bed.

'Mr Stanger was admitted in the night by his son, the
paediatric consultant, Mark Stanger.' There was a
disapproving expression on the matron's face. 'I don't
know why he needed to bring in his own nurse,' she
said, affronted. 'We have excellent nurses, here.' And
she gave Claire a glance that implied doubt that an
agency nurse could cope.

This is all I need, thought Claire—a hostile
colleague.

She looked down at the seriously ill man. The face
that had haunted her dreams was drawn down on the
left side so that it altered his appearance. He did not
look like that man, and her tenseness left her. He was
just another patient. Even when he opened his eyes,
their expression was so vulnerable her compassion
made her smile, but there was little response and no
recognition.

'Nurse Green will show you the charts and give you
the relevant details concerning the patient's treatment.'

The matron nodded towards a dark-haired nurse standing on the other side of the bed.

Claire was glad when the matron departed. Rosemary Green was a pleasant-faced woman, older than Claire.

'I'm only part-time here,' she explained after she had handed over to Claire. 'His blood-pressure is being taken half-hourly now and his pulse every quarter. His temperature is two-hourly for the time being.' She glanced down at John Stanger with a smile. 'His condition is stable.'

'Thanks,' said Claire.

'His swallowing reflex isn't fully restored yet, hence the drip.' Rosemary nodded towards the intravenous infusion of dextrose-saline suspended at the right side of the bed. 'He isn't restless, so that's a good thing.' She patted John's good arm.

After Nurse Green had left, Claire took his readings, noting the increased pulse-rate and attributing this to the nurse changeover. Just because the patient did not respond it did not mean that he was unaware of what was going on.

'It's all right, Mr Stanger,' she said, smiling gently and bending closer to her patient so that he could see her face. 'Just try to relax. You're doing fine, so don't worry.' Her tone was confident.

The anxiety left his eyes and he closed them.

Claire was just recording his blood-pressure when Mark came in. She was all ready to be cross with him for his deception, but it was not the pristine, elegant doctor that she had come to love who approached the bed; it was a worried son whose clothes were unpressed and whose shirt was creased. He looked older than his thirty-five years, and Claire's heart went out to him. He did not even smile at her; his gaze was for his father. He put a hand out and she gave him the charts.

'How is he?' Even the timbre of his voice had altered; it had deepened with anxiety.

'Holding his own,' said Claire in a low voice. 'He's sleeping now.'

'Are you sure it's sleep and that he's not unconscious?' asked Mark, giving her a sharp look.

Claire did not resent his questioning of her ability. She knew it was his anxiety speaking. Pointing to the charts, she said, 'It's all there.'

Mark's body sagged. 'I've not slept.' He rubbed his eyes with his hand. 'I've been so worried.'

'Look, why don't you go home and have a rest?' she touched his arm. 'I'll look after him.' Her tone was gentle — soothing.

Mark covered her hand with his. 'I know you will, and thank you for coming.' He frowned with embarrassment. 'I'm sorry I asked Jessie to recommend you, but you're the best nurse I know, and I felt you didn't like my father.' They had moved away from the bed. His frown deepened. 'I thought you might refuse if you knew who the patient was.' He smiled a little. 'And I had to have the best.' The compliment thrilled her.

But his other words were so true that Claire felt ashamed, and blushed. 'My feelings don't come into it,' she said, then realised her choice of words had been unfortunate when she saw anger leap into Mark's eyes. 'Your father is a patient,' she added lamely, which did not help.

'Why. . .?'

Claire was saved from explaining something she did not want to by a moan coming from the bed. They both hurried to John Stanger's side. Blue eyes, the colour of his son's, looked up at Mark with a helpless appeal.

Claire pushed a chair forward, and Mark sat down.

'Thanks,' he said, not looking at her; his eyes were on his father. 'Don't worry, Dad,' he said, 'you're going to be all right.' But the doctor who could convey confidence by a word or a gesture to his patients was unable to hide his anxiety from his father. It was to Claire that the sick man's eyes moved.

She smiled and touched the unparalysed hand. 'You must believe your son, Mr Stanger.' Her voice was low, her eyes compelling. 'He's telling you the truth.'

Mr Stanger opened his mouth, but no sound came, only saliva dribbled from the affected side. Claire quickly mopped it with a tissue.

Mark seemed to have regained control of himself for he said in a firm voice, 'All you have to do is rest.' His eyes had lost their anxiety. Claire's confidence had brought his father's illness into perspective.

John closed his eyes, and Mark gestured for Claire to join him out of his father's hearing.

The light in the room was dim, just enough for the nurse to see to perform her duties. It was shadowy where they stood, only Claire's white dress stood out in the gloom; Mark was almost invisible. It was like talking to a ghost, and Claire shivered.

He took her hand in his. 'Thanks,' he whispered, 'for restoring my equilibrium.' Claire could not see his face clearly, but she heard the unsteadiness in his voice. She released her hand and took his in both her own, holding them tightly.

'It happened so quickly,' he murmured. 'How human we are, we doctors. We aren't the impersonal people the patients think. We feel as much as any of their relatives.'

'I know.' Her voice was as low as his. 'But you must be strong, for your father's sake.' How many times had she said something similar to the patient's relatives? But now it had an added significance.

'One good thing's come out of this anyway,' he said. 'I'll see more of you.' He drew her close to him, and she did not resist—she couldn't. All those crazy thoughts she had been having vanished as if they had never been. Just the touch of his hands on her arms melted her. How she had missed this simple contact — hand on hand, arms about each other. Thoughts that she could not marry him because his father figured in her dream were forgotten.

'We'll have to put our wedding off until my father's better, sweetheart. Do you mind?' His voice was soft and seductive.

Swept by emotion, Claire whispered, 'No.'

With a soft kiss on her willing lips, Mark left her, assuring her that he would return later.

Claire continued her vigil, and, as she did so, all her fear of the man in the bed slipped away, so that she wondered if she had imagined the dream.

As day followed day and John became stronger, a rapport developed between them. He was so like Mark in many ways — a turn of the head, an expression. It became obvious to her that even though this man was identical to the man in her dream, he could not possibly be that man. Mark's father was not capable of frightening anyone.

Within a fortnight John Stanger was moving his left arm and had some feeling in his left leg. The physiotherapist and the speech therapist had been in constant attendance. With Claire's encouragement, John progressed rapidly.

Three weeks later, Mark came in with the medical consultant, Dr Adam Cooper, a man built like a rugby player.

'You're progressing very well, Mr Stanger,' he said, acknowledging Claire with a nod. 'I think we'll be able to send you for convalescence next week.'

John's eyes brightened, but he did not speak. His speech was not very good.

'Do you have anyone at home, Mark?' the doctor asked.

'No, but my financée will be happy to look after my father,' said Mark with a twinkle in his eye. He was pleased that Claire had overcome her dislike of his father and felt confident in offering her services.

Dr Cooper gave Mark a doubtful glance. 'Perhaps you'd better ask her first.'

'That's easily done.' Mark grinned and looked at Claire. 'What do you think, Miss Forrest?'

Claire smiled. 'I'm sure she'd be very willing.'

Dr Cooper raised an eyebrow. He sensed there was something more here than he knew.

Mark laughed. 'I'd like to introduce you to my fiancée, Adam,' he said, taking Claire's hand and drawing her forward. 'Claire Forrest.'

Adam Cooper's laugh was quiet for such a large man.

'Congratulations,' he said, and shook their hands.

He asked when the wedding was to be, and, when told it had not yet been arranged, said, 'Well, don't forget to put me on your wedding list.'

After the medical man had left, Mark took Claire's hand. 'I rather put you on the spot there. I hope you didn't mind.'

'Of course not.' Claire's smile reassured him. 'It'll be very convenient. I can sleep at home and pop up first thing in the morning.'

'Hm, I suppose that would be best.' He grinned. 'Under my roof all the time would be too much of a temptation.'

'I knew you'd understand,' she said with a laugh, and bent to tuck John Stanger's rug more firmly round his legs to hide her blushes.

The chair was in the window overlooking the hospital grounds. The leaves had fallen from the trees, leaving the branches stark against the grey sky.

John had his eyes closed. Looking down at his father, Mark whispered, 'I'll see you tomorrow.'

He gave Claire a quick kiss on the cheek and left her wanting more.

Mark arrived early on the morning his father was to leave the hospital. After their goodbyes to the staff, he helped Claire settle his father into a hatchback Metro he had borrowed. It accommodated the wheelchair in the boot.

It was a cold November day. Claire pulled the rug up to John's chin and tucked it round his shoulders, shoulders so much thinner than his son's. Her face was close to his and when she saw the anxiety in his eyes she said,

'You'll be fine.' And when the doubt persisted, she smiled and said, 'Mark and I will *see* that you are.'

Tears of weakness rimmed his eyes, and she impulsively kissed his cheek.

'Hey!' Mark's voice came from behind her. 'I'm the Stanger you should be kissing.'

Claire stood up and turning, kissed his cheek and laughed, but he put his arms around her and kissed her on the mouth.

'None of those namby-pamby kisses for me,' he said, releasing her.

Claire laughed.

When they arrived at the flat Mark helped her put his father to bed.

'It's just for a little while,' she promised, seeing the protest in his eyes. 'I'll get you up in an hour,' and she gave him a special smile.

His bed had carved leaves across the top of the smooth mahogany. The modern duvet looked out of place. A more sumptuous covering would have been more fitting. The rest of the furniture matched the bed. The carving was expertly done, and Claire had seen similar pieces in her grandmother's house. The carpet was pale green with a delicate Chinese pattern in pink and greens. There was an Eastern flavour about the whole room. Even the ornaments were from Indonesia. Claire recognised these as well; her grandfather had acquired similar ones on a tour as a marine engineer.

Claire wondered if John Stanger had similar reasons for procuring his collection, but the thought slipped away as she went to join Mark in the lounge.

'I think, while your father's recovering from his trip home, I'll go and unpack,' she told him.

Mark jumped up from the couch. 'I'll carry your suitcase for you,' he said, smiling cheekily.

Claire grinned. 'I think someone should stay with your father,' she said.

His smile broadened. 'We'll tell him we'll only be a moment. He won't worry now he's in a place he knows.'

When they looked in on John he was asleep, so they slipped away quietly.

They had just entered the flat when the bell went. It was Steven. He came into the hall without an invitation.

'I suppose you're going to tell me you were specialling a patient again and that was why I was unable to contact you,' was his disgruntled greeting. Then he saw the suitcase. 'Jumping the gun, are we? Away with your lover?'

Before Claire could answer, Mark had grasped Steven by his shirt-front and pulled him so close to himself that their faces were only inches apart.

'We don't all get up to your tricks,' he snapped, his tone as hard as his face.

Steven had never been a coward. 'So she told you,' he said as he forced Mark's hands away, a sneer on his face.

Mark did not answer, just a slow smile spread over his face. It held a hint of mockery which infuriated Steven. He wanted to hit this man who had replaced him in Claire's affections, and clenched his fists. Then he thought of another way to wreak his revenge, less violent, but equally deadly.

His fists relaxed and he said in a smooth voice, with a raised eyebrow, 'Has she told you about the dream?'

Mark was nonplussed. He had been preparing himself to parry a blow. 'What dream?' he queried.

'No!' Claire's face was stricken. The reasons for not telling him were still the same, for, even though his father no longer held any terror for her, she could not explain the dream. How could she, when she did not know the reason for it herself?

She looked at Mark helplessly and at her cousin pleadingly.

Steven ignored her beseeching look. His pride and vanity had been hurt, and he wanted to strike back. With a wicked glint in his eye, he said, 'I see that I shall have to enlighten you.' The sky outside had darkened, casting his face into gloom. It dirtied his fairness, and to Claire it seemed to herald disaster.

'Claire. . .' Steven paused, then a malicious smile crossed his face '. . .had this dream. A man leans over her threateningly. He's dressed in white. . .' another pause to build the tension. Steven was enjoying himself '. . .rather like a doctor's coat. The man in the dream. . .' His eyes gleamed '. . .was you!' He flung out his arm dramatically, pointing at Mark.

The violent reaction he expected was not forthcoming.

'Really?' said Mark in a dismissive tone. He crossed to Claire and putting his arm round her trembling shoulders said. 'A lot of people look like me.' His face was full of concern as he looked down at her. 'I'm glad I know,' he said gently. 'It explains so many things.' His eyes were not critical; they were loving. Tears slipped down her cheeks — tears of gratitude. She should have trusted him and told him herself.

'Do you still have the dream?' He spoke as if Steven was not there.

Peeved that his words had not had the reaction he had thought, Steven said, in a sneering voice, 'Yes. Do you?'

Claire ignored her cousin. Her eyes were on Mark as she said, 'Not since I met you.'

Defeated, Steven turned. Mark held the front door open for him. As he made to leave, Claire touched his arm. He paused, and it was the old Steven who looked down at her. He had remarkable powers of resilience.

He smiled. It was as if, having purged himself at Claire's expense, he was his old self again. He shrugged.

'Sorry.'

'Keep in touch,' she found herself saying. He had that effect on her. She always forgave him.

Steven nodded and was gone.

Claire leant against Mark as he shut the door. He held her close, smoothing her hair, but he did not speak, just let her weep, her tears dampening his shirt.

When she finally raised her face to his, he wiped her tears away with his finger, then bent to kiss her.

'We'll get married as soon as my father's well enough to attend the ceremony.' He grinned. 'Until then, this must do,' and he kissed her again.

Claire responded so willingly, feeling set free now that he knew about the dream, that his kiss deepened. Her arms tightened about his neck and she clung to him, sensations chasing sensations, rising — rising, until Mark had to release her, otherwise. . .

'Soon, darling, soon,' he murmured.

She was loath to see him go, but knew it had to be so. His father was far from well.

CHAPTER ELEVEN

IT WAS not until the end of November that Mark's father was well enough for the wedding plans to be made.

Surprisingly, Steven had remained in Whiteleigh. At first, when he had contacted Claire, she had been a little worried. He was so changeable, she never really knew where she was with him. But his, 'I'm tired. I want a rest from travelling,' satisfied her that she was not the reason for his staying.

Hazel was delighted when Claire asked her to be her bridesmaid. 'We're having a register office wedding,' Claire told her, 'as neither of us belongs to a church. Steven will give me away.' They were having coffee at the Copper Kettle as she spoke.

Hazel's green eyes became greener with delight.

'Good.'

'You're fond of him, aren't you?' said Claire, picking up a biscuit, and knew she was right when Hazel blushed.

'It's pretty obvious, isn't it?' Hazel laughed without embarrassment, then finished her coffee in a gulp.

Maybe Hazel was the right person for Steven, thought Claire. Her friend would not let him influence her.

'I must see what I can do about throwing you two together,' said Claire, and laughed before finishing her coffee.

'We — well——' Hazel hesitated, then said in a rush, 'I don't think you need to do anything like that. I'm seeing him this evening.'

Should she suggest that Hazel dress in a more

sophisticated way? wondered Claire, surveying her friend's green corduroy skirt and cotton shirt of the same colour.

Hazel saw the doubt in Claire's eyes and guessed the reason for it. 'He'll just have to take me as I am,' she grinned.

Claire laughed. 'You're absolutely right.'

John Stanger did not require Claire's attention continually now. She just helped him to dress in the morning and to undress at night.

The wedding was on December the first.

A week before this date, Jessie Watson rang Claire.

'The agency suggested I phoned you,' she said. 'I'm desperate for staff—the flu's taken its toll. Could you possibly come in?'

Jessie had been very good to Claire. She had insisted on helping to arrange the wedding, so Claire felt she could not refuse.

'Yes, I can come in,' she said.

When she reported for duty at one o'clock, Jessie exclaimed, 'Am I glad to see you. We've been run off our feet. An appendicectomy's in Theatre now and due back any moment.' She sounded decidedly frazzled. 'Another burns case —— Child put her hands on the oven door which was hot after her mother had baked.' An exasperated frown lined Jessie's forehead. 'There should be a printed warning on all oven doors to alert parents. Washing-machine doors get hot as well and all these doors are at the right height for toddlers.' She sighed. 'The child's coming up from Casualty any moment.' Then her face broke into a smile. 'But there's a bright side to all this. Guess who's back?'

Claire did not need to think for long. 'Jimmy Grayson,' she said with a smile.

Jessie laughed. 'Right first time.'

Jimmy Grayson was eleven years old and one of

those boys who was accident-prone. He had fallen out of a tree and smashed his leg quite badly.

'What's he done now?' asked Claire in a resigned voice.

'Nothing, thank God,' said Jessie. 'He's been admitted for physiotherapy.' Her face clouded. 'His leg's not as strong as it should be.'

Claire frowned. 'I thought he was to attend the physio department after school?'

Jessie pulled a face. 'Should have, but he played truant.' Her expression became serious. 'It's not altogether his fault. His parents both work and don't come home until five-thirty. His older brother's sixteen and couldn't care less. That's why he's been admitted.'

Claire nodded. It was the old story.

'Hi, Staff.' Jimmy's cheerful face looked up as Claire went into the ward. He was playing a game of Monopoly with two of the older children, and Claire could see that he had acquired quite a few properties.

'Going to be a tycoon, I see, when you grow up.'

She crouched down beside him.

'Yes.' His simple answer was given with a direct look from a serious face. 'I intend to be a millionaire.'

Claire believed him. There was nothing wrong with Jimmy's intelligence. 'Well, you'll be a limping millionaire if you don't practise your exercises,' she told him with a smile.

'I hadn't thought of that.' He frowned. 'Thanks, Staff.' Then, turning to his companions, he said, 'Can we carry on this game later? I'd better do as Staff says.'

'OK, Jimmy,' said Sandra, a girl of twelve who had her left arm in a sling. 'But I'm going home at three o'clock.'

'I'll be back in an hour,' Jimmy promised.

Two days later, Claire was walking Jimmy back from the physiotherapy department when they met Mark coming out of the pharmacy.

'Hi, Doc,' Jimmy grinned cheekily.

'Well, Jimmy, how's the leg?' Mark smiled down at the youngster with the crew-cut hair.

'Coming along, Doc.' And Jimmy did a little jig to prove it.

'Hey!' Mark caught hold of his arm. 'No larking about.' His face was serious. 'You don't want to undo all your hard work.'

'No,' said Jimmy, trying to measure his stride to the big man's.

Mark laid his hand on the boy's shoulder. 'You should take up swimming,' he said. 'That would strengthen the muscles in your leg.'

Jimmy grinned. 'That's what the physio said, but I can't swim.'

Mark glanced at Claire. 'Perhaps we can do something about that. How about my giving you some lessons? I'm sure Staff will come along to encourage you.'

Claire smiled. It was a little strained, but a genuine smile. 'Indeed I will,' she said, looking at Jimmy, but avoiding Mark's eyes.

The big man's eyes twinkled. 'But it will have to wait a couple of weeks,' he told Jimmy. 'Staff and I have an important engagement to fulfil first.' And the smile he gave Claire was so meaningful that she blushed.

'I know what that is—I know what that is,' sang Jimmy excitedly. 'You're getting married.'

'Right first time, Jimmy,' smiled Mark. He stopped outside the X-ray department. 'I have to leave you here.' He glanced down at Jimmy. 'I won't forget.'

'Thanks, Doc,' the boy grinned.

Claire was kept busy for the rest of the day. The phone was ringing as she put the key into the door at seven-thirty, and she dropped the bag of food she had bought in the supermarket on the way home and lifted the receiver. It was Steven.

Claire had not seen him since that day he had told Mark about the dream, though she had spoken to him on the phone to make the wedding arrangements.

'I was wondering if you and Mark are free to join Hazel and me for dinner on Thursday evening. It will give us a chance to finalise the wedding arrangements.' And Steven mentioned the restaurant where he and Claire had first seen Mark with Susie, the Haven.

'That'd be lovely,' said Claire and meant it. She did not want any friction between them. 'I haven't seen you for ages.'

'I'm sorry, Claire,' her heart lifted at the genuineness in his voice, 'but I've been quite busy.' There was a slight pause, then he said, 'I've gone back to school.' He gave an embarrassed laugh. 'I'm taking a course at. . .' he mentioned a technical college in London '. . .in computer studies.'

Claire was so surprised that she was speechless.

'I thought that would surprise you.' She had never heard such energy in Steven's voice before. 'Imagine your lazy cousin working, and I've Hazel to thank. You know what an enthusiastic person she is — well. . .' He had no need to continue. Claire could imagine Hazel firing Steven with her zeal. She only wished she was like that. Oh, she had lost much of her negativeness in the confidence of Mark's love, but. . .but. . . And the dream did not trouble her any more, but. . .but. . . The memories that lay deep inside her would not let her become a whole person.

She shivered, and pushed such thoughts aside.

'I'm delighted to hear your news.'

'I've a lot to tell you when we meet,' he said, sounding years younger. 'Would eight o'clock suit you?'

'Fine. I know Mark's free that evening.' They had been going to dine out themselves that day.

Claire replaced the receiver and stared at it thoughtfully. How Steven had changed. Surely it was time for her to face her past? She filled the kettle and plugged it in.

She had thought of consulting a psychiatrist, and had suggested it to Steven, but he had pooh-poohed the idea.

'It'll go on your medical records,' he had warned, and she had let him influence her.

The only way for her now would be to relive that time, but——

'No!' She jumped up from the stool, her heart hammering. 'I can't.'

Restlessly she paced the small kitchen, small enough for a prison. Like the prison of my mind, she agonised.

Leaving the kitchen, the tea unmade, she went into the lounge and switched on the television. One of her favourite films was showing, but as she watched it she despised herself for her lack of courage.

On Thursday evening the dinner party was a success. Claire had never seen Steven look so boyish. She was amazed at how he did not mind the way Hazel was dressed. The redhead had on a green velvet frock which fitted and yet didn't quite. Claire knew Steven hated velvet and his eyebrows would have vanished out of the top of his head if she, Claire, had worn it, but he did not seem to notice Hazel's appearance; his eyes hardly left the girl's face.

Claire had chosen an outfit which she knew would please Steven—he had picked it for her himself. It was a two-piece in pale grey brocade with a muted pattern. The top was fitted, the skirt straight. It was smart and elegant. It was a living lie—rather like myself, she thought, catching a glimpse of herself in the restaurant's mirror. Even Mark's, 'You look gorgeous,' when he collected her could not dispel her discomfort, and she wished she had put on the simple black dress she had bought just recently.

When Mark and Claire arrived at the Haven, Steven and Hazel were already there. They looked so happy, Claire thought they seemed to be the ones about to be married instead of Mark and herself.

Later during the evening when Mark was dancing with Hazel, Steven said, 'Excited?'

'Not as excited as you seem to be.' She did not want to give him a direct answer. Apprehension had gripped her. Was she being fair to Mark?

'You noticed.' Steven was happy to be sidetracked, his eyes on Hazel. Then he looked at his cousin. 'Pity Mum and Dad can't be here, but it's impossible for them to leave.'

'Yes,' said Claire. She would miss her aunt and uncle, but she knew how important their trip to America was. 'Never mind—you're here.' She smiled at him.

Steven grinned affectionately at her. 'Hazel's been the making of me,' he told her. Then, nodding in Mark's direction, he added, 'As your doctor will be of you.'

'Yes.' Claire smiled up at Mark, who had joined them, with Hazel.

'Dance?' Mark was holding out his hand to her with a smile that was for her alone—warm, loving.

'Yes, please.' Her eyes were shining as she went into his arms.

It was easy to forget her apprehension when he looked at her with such warmth. He held her close, his arms around her, hers around him, their bodies touching, their cheeks brushing. She was filled with excitement.

They had been so engrossed in each other that they had not noticed the couple dancing beside them.

'Hi, Mark! Hi, Claire!' It was Susie, with a handsome young man. 'Congratulations,' she smiled. 'I can never thank you enough for your kindness.' Turning to the young man, who was appraising Mark, she said, 'This is the doctor I was telling you about, Peter.' Peter's expression turned to one of admiration.

Other dancers jostled them, preventing further conversation.

'I'm proud of Susie,' said Mark, sweeping Claire away. 'She has lots of guts. She's a real fighter.'

Was he suggesting that she wasn't? mused Claire, seeing what she thought was criticism in his eyes.

'Sometimes it's easier to face something that can be seen than something that can't,' she said defensively.

Her eyes were so vulnerable that Mark's arms tightened about her.

'Is there something that *you* can't face, my darling?' he whispered, looking down at her with concern.

'Only losing you,' she answered brightly, if a little tensely.

'No fear of that,' he said, his tone light, but his eyes were thoughtful. 'I know something's troubling you, darling, and I wish you'd tell me what it is.' His smile was encouraging. 'But I won't force you.'

'It was just the dream,' she said, hoping her face looked convincing. 'Now that's gone, I'm fine.' Then to lead him away from dangerous ground, she said, 'It's just pre-wedding nerves,' and laughed, not realising how brittle her laugh sounded to Mark. 'You know I thought you were in love with Susie.'

Mark laughed. 'She was part of my rehabilitation programme,' he said. 'Steven told you about that, didn't he?'

'Yes.'

Mentioning Susie as a way of distracting Mark had set Claire wondering, when he had told her about his reason for being with Susie in such a banal way, if she, Claire, was now part of his rehabilitation programme. Would he go as far as marrying her to help her?

The music had stopped and Mark led her back to the

table. Although Claire enjoyed the rest of the evening, there remained that niggling doubt as to Mark's motive for marrying her.

Mark took her home. He kissed her at the door of her flat, but made no move to come in. 'It won't be long now, darling, when we won't have to say good-night and leave each other.'

Suddenly the enormity of what would be expected of her frightened her. Her doubts as to his motives vanished, lost in her realisation that she had not really faced what being made love to by Mark would mean. She was not ignorant of the facts of life, but knowing and experiencing were two different things. If you love someone, nothing else matters, she thought. Then — but would love be enough?

As if sensing her fears, Mark took her into his arms and kissed her, hoping the bodily contact would sweep her anxieties away. 'You have no need to fear me, sweet one.'

But her serious face did not change. It's not you I'm afraid of, she thought. It's me — my inhibitions, my. . . She could not define what it was that was troubling her.

'Are you sure you want to marry me?' she whispered.

Mark's lips came down on hers in a kiss which should have convinced her, but didn't. Had he kissed her so that he did not need to reply? Was he caught in a web of his own making?

'All will be well on Saturday,' he said, his brow clearing. It was just wedding nerves, as she had said, he decided.

She wished she was as confident, and she wanted him to go.

And yet, when he had gone, she wanted him back so that she could tell him of her doubts, tell him of her fears, tell him about her mother. Was it too late? There was still tomorrow, Friday, the day before her wedding.

But when she awoke next morning, her fears seemed ridiculous. She had the day off. Mark phoned as she was dressing to say he would be unable to see her as he had been asked to see a patient in London.

Hazel had taken the day off, so the girls spent it shopping for last-minute accessories. Claire was grateful for Hazel's level-headedness. Sensing her anxieties, Hazel made her friend laugh with tales of the children at school. By the time Claire had spent the evening with Jessie and her husband, she was beginning to look forward to her wedding day.

December the first was a mild, bright day. Claire had chosen a simple white dress in patterned silk and three-quarter sleeves. She wore a pillbox hat of the same material, with a small veil. Even the roses she carried were white, and with her blonde hair, some of the guests thought she looked colourless, but to Mark she appeared virginal — untouched — and his heart swelled with emotion.

Their vows were exchanged, his firmly, hers in a whisper. The kiss he gave her at the end of the ceremony was chaste. He did not want to disturb her beauty. He hoped that, with care and gentleness, he would be able to change the virginal purity of her face, change it to a glowing happiness. His protective instincts were roused when he felt her arm tremble in his as they walked out of the building and stood on the steps for the photographs to be taken.

It all had a feeling of unreality about it. It wasn't until she stood beside Mark to receive their guests at the reception and heard Jessie say,

'Congratulations, Claire — or should I say Mrs Stanger?' that she knew it was fact, not fantasy.

Some of what she was thinking must have shown on her face, for when she glanced up at Mark she saw that thoughtful expression in his eyes. It was gone in a moment, and he said with his arm around her,

'Indeed you must, Jessie. This is Staff Nurse Stanger from now on.'

'But aren't you going to give up nursing?' Jessie asked. She had assumed that Claire would be resigning from the agency.

'I did suggest it,' said Mark, laughing. 'But Claire thinks she's too young to retire.'

'Ah, well. Once the babies come. . .' Jessie smiled, Claire blushed, and Mark laughed.

The reception was held in the function-room in the Haven. The meal was excellent and the wines expensive. Steven's parents had paid for everything.

It was dark by the time the celebrations had finished.

'So you're going to spend your honeymoon in the Bahamas,' said Steven with a twinkle in his eye.

'How did you find out?' laughed Mark.

'Claire was too eager with her denials.' Steven's grin was engaging.

Mark and Claire left the restaurant at eight o'clock. She had changed into a pale blue trouser suit. The colour made her appear cold, and her expression did nothing to belie this; it was reserved and serious. She did not look like a happy bride, but Mark was not worried. He expected her to be nervous.

They headed the car in the direction of London, but, once well away from the restaurant, Mark turned back towards Whiteleigh.

'It was very clever of you to fool Steven like that,' he said with a smile in his voice. The roads were icy and he had to concentrate.

'Yes. I was quite proud of myself.' Claire forced brightness into her tone. Why did she have this feeling of impending disaster?

Mark parked the car well away from the flats.

'In case some of the wedding guests should come this way,' he told her with his arm round her shoulders.

Claire stilled the shiver that threatened. She did not

want Mark to think she was afraid of him — she wasn't. It was something else. . .something. . .

They were spending their week's honeymoon in Claire's flat. Mark thought she would be more relaxed in her own surroundings. His father was staying with his sister in London until after Christmas.

He opened the door and swept her up into his arms carrying her without effort over the threshold before she could take a breath.

'Must keep the tradition alive,' he said, setting her on her feet with a laugh, but he did not release her. 'Welcome home, Mrs Stanger,' he said, kissing her gently on the lips.

Alone with him, Claire felt her doubts did not seem to matter.

'How about a cup of tea?' he said. 'I'll fetch the suitcases while you make one.' He was gone before she could reply.

The tea was made by the time he returned. She could hear him putting their suitcases in the bedroom and visualised them standing side by side, as she would soon be with Mark in the new double bed. She shivered, partly with apprehension and partly with excitement. The milk she was pouring into a small jug spilt as her hand trembled.

'That's nice,' said Mark from the kitchen doorway, noting the delicate china, which had been a wedding present.

He came in and took the tray from her and put it down. She was in his arms in a moment, eagerly accepting his kisses. He swept her up into his arms, and a craving to feel her naked body close to his roused her so that her longing showed in her eyes.

Mark carried her to the bedroom. The décor was a combination of shades of blue with touches of white. Everything blended, but the perfection gave the room an unlived-in appearance. It was negative. There was no life in it, and for a moment Mark paused. Was he too late? Could he revive this beautiful girl with a kiss, like Sleeping Beauty, or was she lost to him, or any man, forever?

Claire, seeing his hesitation, felt her doubts rising. Was he regretting his marriage?

Mark felt the stiffening of her body and laid her on the bed. He sat down beside her, as he had sat that other time at the houseboat.

He looked down at her, his eyes intense. 'Don't be afraid of me, darling,' his voice was rough with emotion. 'I love you, Claire.'

She searched his face and knew it was true. He had not sacrificed himself by marrying her. She saw the anxiety in his face. He was the vulnerable one now. He was waiting for her to declare herself. She had been so wrapped up in her own feelings that she had not thought of him. She was swept with remorse.

Flinging her arms around him, her face close to his, she whispered, 'I love you.' Her eyes were shining. She kissed him, her lips moist on his.

Mark smiled, gently, lovingly as she released him. He did not hurry her, and she, confident in his love, was unafraid. Slowly and with patience, he initiated her into the ways of love. His caresses were more than caresses, they drew from her the paleness of her beauty and roused a fire she did not know she possessed.

Claire felt alive for the first time in her life. It was not until the peak of their lovemaking, when she saw his face above her with the whiteness of the ceiling and the blueness of the walls behind him in the moonlight shining through the open curtains, that terror gripped her and snatched her happiness away.

Seeing the change in her, the fear in her eyes and thinking it was because he had rushed her, Mark fell back on the bed and hid his frustration behind a light laugh.

'Oh, Mark.' She was immediately contrite. 'I'm so sorry.'

He gathered her into his arms. 'It's I who am sorry, my sweet,' he whispered. 'I was too urgent.'

He pulled the duvet over her, but she pushed it away. It had added to her feeling of suffocation.

She buried her head in his shoulder. 'It isn't you,' she whispered. He could only just hear her. 'It's me.' She raised a troubled face to his. 'I shouldn't have married you,' she confessed. 'But I love you so, I just couldn't help but let you marry me. I thought it would be all right.'

Mark wondered what the 'it' could be, but did not say so. He just smiled. 'As long as you love me, and I love you, all will be well in time.' His smile broadened as he smoothed away the furrows in her brow, but they sprang back.

'I can't really explain it myself,' she said, sitting up.

The moonlight held her, painting her pale skin with a silver sheen so that she looked like a statue of eternal youth, enhanced by Mark's skilful brush-strokes. There was a glow about her that had been missing before. Mark knew he would never give up now, no matter how long it took. Be it forever, he would continue to bring his love out of the wilderness in which she had been living for so long.

Feeling his eyes on her, she looked down at him, fearfully at first, for she thought she might have killed his love, but seeing it there in his eyes she said, taking a deep breath, knowing she owed him this,

'My mother was killed when I was three. I was with her at the time.' Mark longed to stop the anguish he could see in her eyes, but knew he must let her continue, for her own sake. He wanted to know, for how else could he help her?

'My father's job took him all over the world; he was an oil man. He was away at the time. My mother and I had been on holiday in France.' Her face became more tense as she paused, her fists were clenched, her nose pinched. Then the words came out in a rush. 'The ferryboat we were returning on capsized.' Her shoulders sagged. 'My mother was drowned, but I was saved.' The sadness in her eyes was heartbreaking.

And have been feeling guilty ever since, thought Mark as he took her into his arms and smoothed her trembling body. 'Was that the. . .?' Here he mentioned the name of the boat, and Claire nodded. Her head was buried in his shoulder, so she did not see the thoughtful expression that crossed his face.

'My father was devastated.' A shudder shook her body. 'I can't bear any weight on me, and I can't bear water over my head.' She started to tremble, and Mark's arms tightened, enfolding her with his warmth.

'No one is going to put you in the water, my darling,' he whispered close to her ear. 'And there are other ways of making love so that my weight won't make you feel suffocated.'

His hands smoothed away the tensions from her body, and in doing so roused the passion that had been quenched when he loomed over her.

With expertise and delicacy, he brought her from her maidenhood to womanhood and swept away the bleakness from her spirit.

When their passion was spent, Claire lay beside him, no longer the pale, almost lifeless beauty she had been. Her skin had the delicate blush of the rose, her eyes the languid sensuality of the satisfied woman.

Mark, seeing her lying in the moonlight, wished he was an artist who could preserve her transformation forever. The sight did not fill him with triumph, it humbled him. This was his love. That he was the instrument that had wrought this change never entered his mind. He thanked God that she had not been beyond his reach.

That night, as Claire lay enfolded in his arms, she tried to convince herself that she had not deceived Mark. It was true that any weight on her made her feel suffocated, but what she had not told him, was that it was his face looming above her that had terrified her, and how could she tell him that?

She slept, and the dream came again, but this time it was Mark's face that looked at her with menace, Mark's eyes that were cold and threatening.

CHAPTER TWELVE

WHEN Claire woke with Mark's arms around her, she realised how ridiculous the dream had been. She removed his arm carefully, but it woke him. Her serious expression puzzled him a little, but he did not show it, just said,

'That's no way to look after a night of love!' and grinned, his grin broadening as his eyes swept over her naked body.

Claire laughed. It was clear to her now that her fears were only in her imagination. She snuggled back into his arms and he pulled the duvet up to their chins.

'I do love you, Mark,' she whispered.

'I had a suspicion that you did,' he laughed.

But as day followed day and the dream came every night with Mark's face grim and cold appearing in it, her response to his lovemaking became less spontaneous.

He was very good with her, understanding and patient, but she sensed his frustration, and this added to her tension.

Her anxiety increased when she found Mark on the phone a couple of times, especially when he rang off abruptly when she came into the hall.

'Problems with a patient?' she asked on the second occasion.

'No. I was phoning to see if Dad was all right.'

Claire was so sensitive where Mark was concerned that she was sure she detected a hollowness in his tone, and wondered if he was telling her the truth.

She was glad when their week's honeymoon was over

and he went back to work. Jessie phoned her on Wednesday the following week.

'I know you weren't planning on returning to work the same time as Mark, but I was wondering if you could help out for a couple of days. Staff Nurse Rogers is off with flu.'

'Of course I will. Do you want me now?' Claire hoped she did not sound too eager.

'Well, if you could come in at two, it would be wonderful.' Jessie sounded relieved. 'I really appreciate it, Claire. I'll tell Mark you're coming, or would you rather speak to him yourself? He's here.'

'Oh. . .' But before Claire could answer Jessie interrupted with,

'Sorry, he's gone.'

'Never mind, I'll leave him a note.' Anxious that her voice should not sound as strained to Jessie as it did to herself, Claire gave a little laugh.

She hoped that her return to work would occupy her thoughts and help to dispel her anxieties. Jessie greeted her with a kiss and a smile.

'You look wonderful,' she said, and laughed when Claire blushed. 'A real advert for marriage.' Then her face became serious. 'We've just admitted a little girl of three years old. She was walking along the promenade with her parents and ran ahead. She climbed on to that little wall, the one that edges the prom.' Claire nodded. 'The tide was high; she wobbled and fell in.' Claire clenched her fists and hid them behind her back.

'Luckily the sea was calm and the father jumped in and rescued her, but she'd swallowed a lot of seawater and was suffering from shock. Ronnie North admitted her for observation. He thinks she might have inhaled some of the water as well.' Jessie smiled at Claire. 'You're so good with these little ones, perhaps you could comfort her. Her mother's there, but she's a bit agitated.' Jessie picked up the notes and handed them

to Claire. 'The child's name is. . .' she laughed
'. . . Claire. I hadn't realised it was the same as yours —
Claire Woodson.'

There was only one page in the folder, and it was
soon read. Claire handed the notes back. 'I'll go and
see her now.'

'She's in the bed just as you go in. On the right,'
Jessie called after her.

Claire drew in her breath sharply when she saw the
small fair-haired child propped up with pillows in the
bed. It could have been herself at that age. The face
was delicate, the eyes the same colour as hers — blue.

A feeling of unreality gripped her, so that all she
could do was stare at the child who was gazing up at
her.

'Staff!' Mark's sharp voice came from beside her.

She looked up at him, but did not see *her* Mark, she
saw the cold face of her dream, and she could not move
or speak. The fear in her eyes was a reflection of the
fear now showing in the sensitive child's.

'Staff!' Mark's voice was severe. 'Pull yourself
together.' He had lowered his voice now, but the
whiteness of his coat, coupled with his fierce eyes, was
so like her nightmare that she felt her senses reel.

He gripped her arm and said in a firm voice, 'Staff
Nurse Forrest, I would like you to help me examine
little Claire, please.'

The use of her maiden name shocked her out of her
nightmare. 'Yes, sir,' she said, her voice a whisper. She
was holding herself stiffly in an effort to control her
dizziness.

'Where's the mother?' muttered Mark, glancing
around.

'Mummy, Mummy.' The child seized on the name,
the small face crumpling in distress.

'I was under the impression she was here.' Claire
spoke with difficulty, her mouth was so dry.

'An impression isn't enough.' Mark was furious. 'You should *know*, Staff.'

It was only by a supreme act of discipline that Claire prevented her face from crumpling like the child's.

Was this the man in whose arms she had lain last night? Her emotions were so disturbed—loving yet hating him—that this attack on her efficiency was too much. She would have given anything to have screamed at him, hit him, left him there in the ward, but she couldn't. Her nurse's training prevented her.

Before she could speak, however, another voice said, nervously, 'I'm sorry I wasn't here. I just went to get my daughter some sweets,' and a fair woman with a small face appeared beside them. She was looking at the angry doctor and the white-faced nurse with apprehension, thinking she was the cause of their displeasure.

Claire, sensing this, smiled. 'We've only just arrived,' she explained, and did not see Mark's rueful expression of apology.

The worry lines on the pretty woman's forehead cleared and she smiled.

'I just want to examine your daughter's chest, Mrs Woodson,' Mark explained.

He sat on the bed and smiled at the child. 'There's nothing to be afraid of, poppet,' he said. 'I'm only going to put this. . .' he showed her the disc at the end of his stethoscope '. . .on to you here.' He touched the child's chest. 'You can hold it if you like.' He held it out. The small child reached for it, attracted by its shape, and a smile lifted the anxiety from the delicate face.

Claire leaned their patient forward and slipped off the nightgown. Quickly Mark sounded the chest and when he had finished gave the small tummy a tickle. The child giggled delightedly, all her fear of the dark man in the white coat had vanished. What a gift he has, thought Claire, and, like the child, her love pushed away her fears.

It was this love that Mark saw when he looked up at her, but he did not betray the pleasure it gave him; his face remained bland. Claire was standing at the top of the bed beside the child, and the similarity between the two impressed itself upon Mark. He became more convinced, then, that he had solved the problem concerning her fears.

He turned to the child's mother. 'Mrs Woodson, you're little one is lucky. She seems to be fine. Her chest's clear, so you can take her home tomorrow. I'll write to your doctor.'

'Oh, thank you, Doctor. We'll never take her near the water again,' Mrs Woodson promised.

'Well, that would be a pity,' said Mark with a smile. 'Think of all the fun she'd miss. Teach her to swim — children of that age swim quite happily.' He looked at Claire. 'Don't they, Staff?'

Her face stiffened. 'I expect you're right, sir,' she said, and expected another disapproving look at her unconvincing reply, but he just nodded.

'I'd like to see you in the office, Staff, when you've dressed the patient.'

'I'll do that,' Mrs Woodson said eagerly.

As Claire walked beside Mark she felt that his white coat distanced him from her somehow. He was no longer her lover, her husband. He was the paediatric consultant. Jessie was busy in the ward and smiled at them as they passed.

The office was empty. Mark took off his white coat and hung it on the back of the door. This helped. Claire steeled herself as he turned, but she relaxed when she saw his concerned expression.

'Claire, darling.' He came and gathered her into his arms, tipping her bowed head back so that he could look into her eyes and saw there the troubled expression he had seen so often before.

'Can't you tell me what the problem is? I know it concerns more than your mother.' He stroked her cheek with the back of his hand. 'Can't you trust me?'

Claire was afraid she would lose his love if she told him the dream was back and that his face in it filled her with fear. She was also worried that his calm acceptance of Steven's revelation about the dream meant that Mark did not believe her cousin, that he had put Steven's outburst down to malice.

Tensing, she pulled away from the comfort of his arms and said, picking up little Claire's notes, 'It's nothing.' She waved the notes, her smile brittle. 'It was just the similarity between this child and myself, that's all.'

Mark's face was unreadable, but his tone as he said, 'Really?' implied that he did not believe her. 'Then I suggest that you make an effort not to allow the past to intrude on your work.'

Claire was stricken. If she told him she might lose him, and if she did not she would. This realisation brought her peace. There was only one thing, then, that she could do. She must tell him the truth, and she was about to when Jessica came into the office.

'A young man's here to see you, Mark,' she said, bringing Jimmy Grayson forward. Then she sensed that it was a bad moment, but there was nothing she could do now. It was too late to draw back.

Mark's stern face relaxed. 'Did you think I'd forgotten my promise, Jimmy?'

Jimmy grinned. 'Yes,' he said cheekily, and Mark laughed. 'How about Saturday? Ten o'clock at the pool.' He glanced at Claire. 'We'll both be there, won't we, Mrs Stanger?'

It was said expressionlessly, with just a raised eyebrow.

It was easy to smile at Jimmy. 'Yes, I'll be there,' she promised.

Mark left the office with Jimmy, and Claire quickly followed, eager to escape Jessie's sympathetic expression. She spent the rest of her time on duty wondering how she would face Mark when she went home.

They were living in her flat. It was a temporary arrangement until they had time to look for a house, but, as Claire put her key into the lock, she wondered if she would ever live in a house with Mark, or anywhere.

The flat was dark. Mark was not there. She glanced at her watch—it was ten-thirty. Where was he? Had he left her? Grief caught at her. And then she saw the note; it was propped up by the phone.

Had to go up to London. I'll be back early Saturday morning. Meet me at the pool.
Mark

Not 'love, Mark', just 'Mark'.

Tears ran down her cheeks, dropped on to the note, dented the paper, distorting the words, twisting them—the way I'm twisted, Claire thought, and blamed herself for marrying Mark. She had only brought him misery.

She was to work on Jessie's ward until the weekend, and she was glad. It would stop her thinking of how her marriage was failing.

By the time Saturday came, Claire had determined that she would tell Mark about the dream, and with this decision made, her mood lightened.

But it was a wan Claire who arrived at the indoor swimming pool at ten o'clock. Mark was waiting for her in the foyer, and just the sight of him filled her with joy. It shone from her eyes. She saw only him. It wasn't until he said,

'Hallo, Claire,' that she noticed his father was standing, almost as tall as his son, on Mark's left.

Even then Claire did not take her eyes from Mark's face. She was searching it, looking for the coldness she had last seen there, and was relieved when she saw only a smile.

'Jimmy couldn't come — he has flu. I thought it would be an opportunity for my father to go in the pool. The pysiotherapist said it would be good for him.'

Claire smiled at Mr Stanger senior and was pleased to see how well he looked. As they walked towards the ticket office, she complimented John on his improvement.

'Yes.' The grey-haired man smiled, still a little crookedly. 'My sister's quite a tartar and keeps me exercising.' Anxiety crept into his eyes. 'I hope this visit won't inconvenience you. Mark's taking me back tomorrow.'

Claire linked her arm through his. 'Of course not. I'm delighted to see you.' And she was. His arrival was helping to relieve the tension building up inside her.

Mark handed her a spectator's ticket and said, 'Sit at the front so you can see us.'

She nodded. She did not want to sit at the front of the spectators' seats. She did not want to be there at all, and had only come because she had promised Jimmy.

Christmas was only ten days away, so there were only a few people in the pool. The majority of the public were shopping for presents.

The water rippled and lapped against the sides of the pool — lap-lap, swish-swish, and Claire shivered, even though the air temperature was high. She did not want to sit in the front row, but she felt she had to.

The two men appeared, and the similarity between

them was marked. Although John was thinner, he was still a well-built man.

They waved to Claire. Then Mark helped his father to enter the water and swam beside him until they were almost level with Claire. They were close enough for her to see their faces, and as they drew near, she thought she detected stress in the older man's features.

Suddenly he held up his hand as if for help. Mark was behind him and did not appear to notice. Without thinking, Claire rushed to the poolside and reached for the outstretched hand. Wet hand grasped dry one, but instead of going with her pull, John Stanger's arm went rigid and unbalanced her. She fell into the water.

Her clothes dragged her down, and her panic made her arms flail. The whiteness of the pool sides, the blueness of the water, and the face — the face in her dream — increased her terror. It was her nightmare. But no. This was real.

Arms grasped her, but she fought them off, tried to beat at the white face, scratch the blue eyes. As they broke the surface, it was John Stanger's face she saw over Mark's shoulders. Mark had deliberately brought her up so that it was his father's face she saw first. It was taut, the eyes were tense, and suddenly everything became clear. The great weight she had been carrying since she was a child of three was lifted from her as Mark helped her from the pool. She realised, now, that the expression she had been terrified of for years was that of a man under stress, not hard and menacing as she had supposed as a child of three. She knew she had imputed the terror *she* had been feeling at that time to the man who was rescuing her.

'Are you all right?' Mark's anxious eyes peered closely at her.

'Yes,' she said, smiling. 'I'm better than I've ever been.'

Her eyes were bright, her voice assured. Her fair

hair clung to her scalp, the wet fringe in streaks on her
forehead. She had taken off her anorak before she fell
in because of the warmth, so she was just wearing jeans
and a jumper. They were moulded to her figure,
outlining her slenderness, and Mark felt a lump in his
throat.

'We must get you changed,' he said with concern,
and made to help her to her feet.

Her hand restrained him. 'No — wait.' She frowned.
'Your father — I don't understand.' She was looking
beyond him, but Mr Stanger senior was not there.

Mark grinned. 'Dad's gone to change.' And when
her frown deepened, he said, 'All will be explained
when you're dressed. I've got a bag of clothes with
me.' He was still grinning. 'I'll hand them to the
attendant in the female changing-rooms.'

Claire was too astonished to speak, and Mark
laughed.

'It was a conspiracy,' was all he would tell her.

She was on her feet now. 'But you can't leave it at
that,' she protested.

'After you've changed.' There was a mischievous
twinkle in his eyes.

'But. . .'

'I'll see you at the entrance,' he insisted.

They were waiting for her when she appeared in a
pair of navy blue trousers and a red jumper which she
had not felt confident enough to wear at the time of
buying. Now she wore the red without thinking, and
somehow it seemed to convey to the two men the
dramatic change in her.

Claire walked betwen the tall silent men.

'Tell me, tell me,' she implored Mark, but he just
grinned and shook his head.

In the car, John Stanger relented and said, 'Will you
forgive us?' He was sitting beside her in the back.

Claire took his hand and smiled. 'I don't really know

what I'm supposed to forgive. I'm a bit confused,' and her smile trembled a little.

John patted her hand. 'Mark wants to tell you himself,' he confided.

'Indeed I do,' said Mark from the driving seat. 'I want all the credit.' There was laughter in his voice.

'Credit for what?'

Mark ignored the plaintive tone in her voice.

'Patience,' he said, and Claire could see him smiling in the driving mirror.

It did not take them long to reach the flat. As soon as they were sitting in front of the fire in the lounge, she demanded, 'Now will you tell me?'

'When we've had a cup of tea,' he said. 'After all, you have had a shock, remember.' His face was serious.

'But I don't feel shocked,' she assured him. 'I feel marvellous. In fact, I can't remember feeling like this before.' She looked amazed. 'It's as if I've been made whole.' Her face had lost the closed, doubtful expression which had recently so worried Mark. It was glowing and alive.

He kissed her on the lips, and when she would have clung to him, no long feeling the barrier which had been there before, he put her gently from him.

'Later,' he promised. 'I'll make the tea.'

He was back with the tea in a few moments. Claire poured.

They had each taken a drink, then Mark said, 'It was your telling me how you and your mother were victims of that ferry disaster that set me thinking.' He took another sip and held his cup in both hands as if to warm them. 'My father. . .' he glanced at John, '. . .was on board that ship. He was one of the officers, and I remember hearing how he'd rescued some of the passengers, among them a child whose mother died. It was in the papers at the time. There was even a photo of the little girl.

'When I saw how small Claire affected you and how frightened you were of me, I put two and two together.' He had been sitting in the armchair, but now came and sat beside her on the couch and took her hand. 'You see, Claire, darling, I know the details of your dream. Steven told me just before we were married. He thought I should know in case. . .' He shrugged, and Claire knew that psychiatric treatment had been in his mind. She smiled encouragingly into his face.

The strained lines that had appeared about his eyes slipped away. 'I thought I'd see how things went with us before I suggested anything in that direction, but when I realised that I was figuring in your dream now, I knew I must take action.' He grinned. 'Hence the pool.' He looked at little sheepish as he said, 'I put Jimmy off, promising to teach him next week. Sorry about the lie, but it was in a good cause.'

Claire gave him a quick kiss, and heartened by this, Mark continued, 'I thought that if you experienced the same happening as an adult that you had as a child and saw my father's face immediately following, you'd understand the reason for your fear, and that the fear was not of my father, but was your own terror at being thrown into the water, separated from your mother.'

He touched her face gently and said softly, 'When you never saw her again the shock left you with this nightmare, and Steven didn't do much to help you. He wanted to keep his influence over you.

'It wasn't until you became engaged to me and he fell in love with Hazel that he admitted to himself what he could have done. That's why he told me about the nightmare in detail.'

The silence which followed his words was complete. No sound disturbed it, no bird cried, no wind blew. The three occupants in the lounge were still. They had the appearance of a painting — Claire in her red jumper the only discordant colour amongst the muted shades of beige décor and the grey suits of the two men.

Then a great sigh escaped her lips. 'I feel as if I've reached the end of a long journey.' She spoke softly, her words falling like petals from a flower.

Mark took her into his arms, his father forgotten, and kissed her lightly on the lips.

'I think it's time I went home,' said John Stanger with a smile.

Mark grinned at him over Claire's shoulder. 'Yes, perhaps it is.'

Claire went with them to London. She could not bear to be parted from Mark even for that short while. It was three o'clock before they had settled John with his sister.

'Won't you stay for a meal?' asked Sheila Stanger, hoping for a chat.

Mark put his arm around Claire. 'No, thanks.' He looked down at his wife, a mischievous twinkle in his eye. 'We have an engagement, haven't we, my sweet?'

Claire's blush was answer enough, but she said, 'Yes.'

'Well, off you go then, but come and visit us soon.'

They promised to do so.

Once in the car, the urgency they had been feeling left them. Their time was their own now, and they wanted to savour it. The stress that had soured their relationship was no longer there. They could relax in each other's company.

The dullness of the day brought the darkness of the night earlier so that they found themselves driving with just the headlights to break the gloom.

The darkened interior of the car enfolded them, drew them closer. As they left the heavy traffic behind and the silence of the road was broken only by the hum of the engine, Claire closed her eyes and slept.

'Wake up, darling. We're home.'

Home. What a wonderful word that was, thought Claire, smiling into Mark's face as he handed her from the car.

'Sorry I slept,' and she was. She did not want to miss a minute of time with him.

'You needed it.' He smiled down at her. 'Remember you've had an emotional shock.' He took her arm and led her towards the entrance. 'I'm very proud of you,' he said giving her a quick kiss.

Claire responded joyfully.

'Hey!' He put her from him. 'Let's wait until we're indoors.' His laugh was husky.

Claire had been so engrossed in Mark that it wasn't until they reached the building that she noticed their surroundings.

'This isn't the flat,' she said, her eyes wide.

He grinned. 'No.' He sounded pleased with himself. 'I booked a room for us here while you were repairing your make-up at Sheila's.'

'How lovely.' Tears edged her lids at his thoughtfulness.

His arms about her, they entered the hotel he had brought her to the day she had fainted.

'Is the houseboat still round the corner?' she asked as they approached Reception.

'It is.'

She detected a touch of anxiety behind his smile.

'I wonder if they're serving dinner,' she said, eager to please him, wanting to show him she was cured.

'I'm sure they do.' He smiled delightedly. Then a small frown appeared between his brows. 'Are you ready for that?'

Claire wasn't quite, but she was determined not to show it and said, 'I'm bound to be all right accompanied by the miracle doctor.' And she smiled.

'Don't tell everybody or they'll be queueing up for

consultations, and we don't want that tonight, do we?' His grin was outrageous.

She laughed.

The houseboat restaurant was owned by the hotel, so Mark had no difficulty in booking a table. It was in their room that Claire wailed,

'But I've nothing to wear.'

'Just you wait there. We'll see what the miracle doctor can do,' and he was gone before she could question him.

He returned a few minutes later with a suitcase. Throwing back the lid, he lifted out her black dress.

'Olé!' he said with a flourish.

Claire flung her arms around his neck and kissed him.

'You're wonderful,' she told him, smiling.

'Of course, but watch out for the dress,' he warned laughing as it was crushed between them.

'Blow the dress,' she said, her arms tightening round his neck, her lips warm on his.

The dress fell to the floor, followed by their clothes, and gave the appearance of a rummage sale.

The double bed was big, with a feather mattress that enfolded them in its embrace. The spirits of other lovers who had slept in this bed filled the room with past happiness and seemed to bless the couple entwined on the bed.

Claire's response was all and more than Mark could desire, and their lovemaking transcended even *their* expectations.

Afterwards, as they lay in each other's arms, Claire whispered, 'Do you think they still have our table?'

He pulled back from her, a grin on his face.

'Hungry?' there was devilment in his eyes.

She laughed. She knew he wasn't referring to food. 'I booked the table for later,' he told her, smiling. 'I suspected something like this might happen.'

'Prepared for every eventuality,' she quipped.

'I was a Boy Scout.'

'Really?' she laughed.

'Yes, really,' he grinned. 'And you're not allowed to laugh at your husband, I shall have to chastise you for that.' He shook his finger at her. 'Very gently, of course,' and his lips touched hers, gently, as he had said, but the lightness of his touch roused such passion between them that their dinner was forgotten.

Some time later they left the room. The black dress enhanced Claire's fair skin. Her blonde hair swung about her face as they walked along the path which joined the hotel with the houseboat.

She drew the short edge-to-edge black jacket more closely about her. It was cold, but this was not the reason she was snuggling into her coat. She was afraid of failing Mark, afraid that her new found assurance would slip away.

As if sensing her anxiety, Mark put his arm round her shoulders and whispered close to her ear, 'I love you.'

She turned a radiant face to his and pressed closer to his side. The path was poorly lit and their shadows blended together, making them one.

'Hey!' His voice was husky as she grinned cheekily up at him.

They walked, arms entwined, across the gangway. Claire was so bewitched by Mark that they were aboard before she realised it.

Their table was beside the window and overlooked the blackness. There was nothing to show they were on a boat; it could have been the hotel.

Claire and Mark were so late that they were soon alone, and it was then that the lap-lap of the water could be heard.

Mark watched the face of his loved one, ready to whisk her away if she showed signs of distress.

Claire reached for his hand. 'It's all right,' she said, and he could see that it was. Her eyes were bright with exuberance. 'Isn't it marvellous?' She glowed with delight. 'It really is all right. I'm not afraid any more.' A softness entered her eyes. 'Thank you, my darling,' she whispered.

Love for her rose and snatched his speech away. She looked so beautiful, but it was not the fine bones of her face or the fairness of her skin, the blueness of her eyes or the silkiness of her hair that made her so. It was the luminous quality which shone from her eyes and seemed to envelop her in a shimmering glory. Mark knew he was being fanciful, but to him she became the stars at night, the moon in the sky, the sun on a summer's day, the snow hanging from the trees in winter. The fact that he had come so close to losing her made her more precious, and he resolved to spend his life making her happy.

They had eaten little, just fruit juice and an omelette. Food had not been important. Claire's stepping on the boat had.

'Let's not wait for coffee,' said Mark, his voice low, his eyes compelling.

Her smile was alluring as he took her hand raising her to her feet. She went willingly. He paid the bill and they left.

The hotel was quiet. Only another couple besides themselves was staying there. The reception desk was unattended and they crept past, not wanting to see anybody; it would spoil the illusion that they were alone.

Their bedroom welcomed them, and Claire resolved to decorate their own bedroom, when they bought a house, in the blue and pink colours of this room to always remind her of her present happiness. In the years to come, if problems beset their marriage, she would always be the first to stretch forth her hand to the man who was looking at her, now, with such love.

Their night was spent in ecstasy, and when they finally slept, it was in each other's arms.

Claire's nightmare never came again.

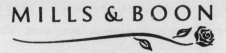

Proudly present to you...

BETTY NEELS' 100ᵀᴴ ROMANCE

Betty has been writing for Mills & Boon Romances for over 20 years. She began once she had retired from her job as a Ward Sister. She is married to a Dutchman and spent many years in Holland. Both her experiences as a nurse and her knowledge and love of Holland feature in many of her novels.

Her latest romance *'AT ODDS WITH LOVE'* is available from August 1993, price £1.80.